Spring's Saboteurs

Books by Andean White

Winter's Thief

Spring's Saboteurs

Spring's Saboteurs

Book 2

ANDEAN WHITE

IC
PRESS

Idea Creations Press
www.ideacreationspress.com

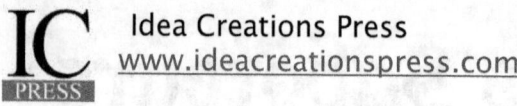 Idea Creations Press
www.ideacreationspress.com

Code for free maps: WT2014

Library of Congress Control Number: 2015948989

ISBN-13: 9780996665711
ISBN-10: 0996665714

Printed in the U.S.A.

Dedication

This book is dedicated to my parents and co-parents—LaNeil, Robert, Mary, and Silvio. They have been an endless source of support—encouraging, editing, suggesting, promoting, distributing, and sparking ideas - a short list of their many contributions.

Thank you.

Acknowledgements

Many thanks to Kathryn Jones of Idea Creations Press for redistributing the commas, keeping the book tense...I mean, correcting the verb tense, and removing the occasional hyphen. Thanks Kathryn for your professionalism and keeping it fun.

Thanks to Nate Paret for taking my stick drawing and turning it into an artful book cover.

A book does not get printed, or digitized without a technical expert. Doug Jones takes a dozen files, a manuscript, and cover images—melds them together and a book appears.

A special thanks goes to the beta-readers for their quick and thoughtful feedback—Cindy Paret, Kim Logan, LaNeil Andes, Lynda Logan, Mary Zancanella, Melanie Nish, Robin White, and Robert Andes.

I could not write this book without the medications and timely decisions of Dr. David Shprecher DO, Meghan S. Zorn PA-C, and the many other professionals at the University of Utah Movement Disorders Clinic. Thank you!

White Knuckles

The warm air pockets carried on the light breeze reminded Reginald of an October harvest. It was a momentary relief from the morning chill of an early spring day.

Why is my life so unrewarding, he thought staring down at the cobblestone street.

"Will we be late for church?" Elsa asked.

"We are not the last members on the street," Erma replied.

"Hopefully, we will not have to sit on the front bench."

Reginald picked up the pace. Like Elsa, he did not want to pass the congregation to the open seats up front.

He missed farming, fishing, trapping, and most of all the tremendous satisfaction of a good harvest. He missed the old Reginald—strong, confident, capable, and happy. Now he had an unfulfilling desk job as the Minister of Farming.

The twins tugged on his coat sleeves.

"Father, you are hurting my hand," Elsa said.

"Yes. Me too," Erma added.

He shook his head, knelt on one knee, and looked into the eyes of the twins in their yellow and white spring dresses.

"I am sorry. I was not paying attention," he said, clearing his throat.

"Are we going back to the farm?" Erma asked.

A noise similar to hail falling on a wooden slat roof filled the maze of narrow streets—unusual for a Sunday morning. Reginald checked the street in both directions. He returned his attention to the girls.

"What brings about that question?" he asked.

"We heard you talking with mother last night," Elsa replied.

"Would you like to return to ..." He looked over his shoulder as the noise sharply elevated.

Reginald focused on the six horses galloping on the cobblestone street towards them. He stood quickly and gently guided the twins to the street's edge.

The Long Bow Knights had the right of way. The knight on the left carried the Manshire flag. Riding high in the saddle, the Long Bows looked regal and smart in their olive and light brown uniforms.

He glanced to check that his daughters were safe then returned his attention to the six horsemen. The twins had covered their ears.

Something is not right. He placed an arm in front of each twin.

The other lead knight held up his hand and the detail stopped. Sparks flew momentarily from the horseshoes sliding on the cobblestones.

"Grab the girls!" the knight said.

The two middle Long Bow knights dismounted their horses and ran toward the twins. Reginald stepped toward the closest knight while pushing his girls behind him. His heart was beating violently and his hands shaking uncontrollably.

"You cannot do this. Do you know who we are?" Reginald asked. His eyes widened. "Where are your green collar bars? You are not Long Bow Knights. Who are you?"

A horseman, in the last pair of rogue knights, moved close to Reginald and the sudden movement diverted his attention. In the time it took a hummingbird's wings to flap, the horseman had struck him with a sword's pommel.

Time moved slowly for Reginald after that. He heard the girls' screams, shook his head to keep from passing out, and felt the agony of a helpless father. The physical hurt migrated in his head. His focus was impaired. Reaching for the closest girl he caught the rogue knight's arm. The knight jerked free of Reginald's grasp.

The screaming was louder and his daughters called out for their father. He shook his head again and clarity replaced the cloudy thoughts. Again, Reginald reached for his daughter and felt the scab on her knee from the fall last week.

The rogue knight had turned toward Reginald as his fist struck the kidnapper on the cheek. He prepared for a second punch.

Reginald's eyes blurred and a sharp pain spread from the top of his head. Time stopped as he twisted to the ground.

His daughters were being carried away. If only I was stronger. He heard the screaming, tasted the salt from the dripping blood, felt the cold cobblestones through his pants. The last image he recalled was their yellow and white dresses.

* * *

Kendrick briskly rubbed his hands together, exposed his palms to the orange, black, and grey cinders giving off their last reserves of heat. A few embers escaped the hearth as he quietly placed another log on the coals.

Early spring meant the floor chilled his feet as he walked past the bed, and the chair holding his weapons. He thought about wearing his boots, but decided the noise might wake his sick wife. He momentarily watched her sleep. I hope the rest of our marriage is as fulfilling as the past two years. It is good to be the queen's husband.

Kendrick rubbed his curly brown hair as he approached the window. He softly placed his warm hands on the chilly metal latches, slowly opening the natural chestnut shutters to reduce the squeak of the hinges.

It was early morning. Bees would be buzzing from bloom to bloom shortly. The morning sun ascended above the rolling horizon defined by the far off hills. The trees stretched toward the sun's first rays, which accented the uppermost quaking leaves.

The birds' melodic chirping momentarily replaced the gentle rippling water of the moat. A couple of woodpeckers drummed their song on a large tree. The rose bush leaves had begun to bud.

The peaceful moment was abruptly disturbed by six galloping horses—with what appeared to be Erma and Elsa—the queen's younger twin sisters. He watched, momentarily confused, before walking to the bedside.

"Althea, wake up," Kendrick said. "Are your sisters scheduled for a ride or anything outside the castle today?"

She groaned, rolled over in bed, and pushed her disheveled blonde hair away from her face.

"What?" Kendrick watched as she blinked repeatedly then rubbed her eyes.

He repeated his question slower and louder hoping she would hear it and understand. "Are Elsa and Erma scheduled for any activity outside the Castle?"

"NO, no. It is Sunday."

A strong knock startled them; Kendrick looked to Althea who was already watching him. They focused on the door. Kendrick moved toward his weapons.

"Kendrick. Kendrick!" came the shout from outside the door.

The thick oak door eerily squeaked. Reginald, foregoing any queen's protocol, glanced over his shoulder before entering. His face was the color of day old snow. From the draft off the door, Kendrick could smell Reginald's sweat. Blood dripped down his temple and dribbled off his chin staining his shirt. Kendrick thought Reginald acted like a drowning man who might at any moment burst from the long deep gasping. After a few moments, he was able to speak.

"Six men—dressed as Long—Bows kidnapped—the twins—as we—walked to church—you must help—me get my— daughters back."

He had never witnessed Reginald's anger. White knuckles outlined the fists. Kendrick wondered if they had been clinched since the kidnapping.

"Yes, yes—come. We will gather some knights and rescue the twins," Kendrick said. He placed his arm around Reginald's shoulder. "Here, use this to stop the bleeding." Kendrick handed him a shirt and pointed toward a chair.

Althea sat up on the side of the bed. "Did they hurt my sisters? I will see that the kidnappers are hunted and punished for taking the twins."

Kendrick's eyes widened as he looked to Althea. He had grown used to a soft, tired voice of late. Queen Althea put on her robe and shoes. She gasped when she noticed Reginald holding a shirt against his head. "Are you alright, Father?"

An uncomfortable silence filled the room. Kendrick and Althea glanced at each other waiting on Reginald to reply.

"Sorry. I have to remind myself that you are the adopted princess of the former king, but my daughter by birth. I'll be fine, but cannot be certain about the twins. Before fainting, it seemed the kidnappers did little to stop the screaming."

"You two, go to the stables and saddle the horses. I will notify the captain of the Long Bows," Althea replied.

"To the stables." Kendrick reached for the oak door and raced through the hallways—he could hear Reginald's smacking boots. He passed the marble statue of the former King Louis III, the portrait of Louis III with Queen Elizabeth, and three tapestries the queen had received as gifts from the king.

"How did you know they were not Long Bows?" Kendrick asked.

There was only silence. He turned to discover Reginald had stopped. Reginald was breathing heavily, his eyes staring at the floor, his hands gripping the thigh muscles above his knees. Kendrick rolled his eyes. Rescuing the twins was going to be difficult and slow. He walked briskly toward Reginald.

"How did you know they were not Long Bows?" Kendrick asked after Reginald's breathing had calmed.

"I was too late in noticing— but they did not have any bars — sewn on their collars." Reginald inhaled quickly.

"What happened?"

"They were galloping down the street then suddenly stopped in front of us. At that moment I realized they were not Long Bows. One hit me with his sword handle and dazed me. Before I could react, my girls were gone."

"Will you be okay? Do you think you can ride a horse and keep up?"

"Kendrick, I will do what is needed to rescue my daughters."

"We are almost at the stables." As he pointed, he said, "I will meet you outside by that door after gathering the horses."

"Go, I will be fine," Reginald said.

Kendrick exited the door and joined the seven Long Bows running toward the stables. Oscar, captain of the Long Bows, one of the queen's most trusted knights, was waiting on his horse as the others gathered their supplies.

Kendrick made eye contact as Oscar nodded.

"The sergeant and four men are guarding Queen Althea," Oscar said.

Oscar, Kendrick, Reginald, and seven knights raced through the main gate after the kidnapped Erma and Elsa.

The kidnappers were about forty minutes ahead.

* * *

From behind the large boulders, Lieutenant Charles Cromwell occasionally pinched his nose, watching as the ten men rode out the castle gate. Waiting until the galloping hooves faded to silence, he hiked up the steep hillside grabbing small trees and fresh grass to assist his climbing. In the clearing behind the crest of the hill, his three men and five horses waited for instructions.

"Oscar and Kendrick are gone with the father and seven knights. We can enter the city now. Remember, act calm, like we live here," Charles said.

"Aye, lieutenant," they replied.

Charles's head jerked back rapidly and was accompanied with a quick breath. Summer was nine weeks away. He hoped this sneezing would cease. If not, such a small inconvenience could unravel the plot ordered by his king.

* * *

14

Althea had been ill for six days. Her natural mother had been sick about three days, and the queen's chambermaid would return tomorrow after recuperating from lung fever the past week.

Today was the worst—thanks to the kidnappers. She had managed to keep a pleasant demeanor with everyone, so far.

Knowing she would need sustenance (the queen was always on duty), she managed to chew a few bites. Althea distorted her face with each bite, rubbed her growling stomach, and then wiped the sweat from her forehead. Eating in her bedroom helped maintain her dignity—in case the food disagreed with her.

Today she had tested walking around the castle halls hoping to settle her stomach before eating the rest of her meal. She walked by the statue of her stepfather, the painting of her stepparents, and the three tapestries cherished by her stepmother.

Her shoulders slumped, and she scuffed her shoes as she walked for nearly an hour, wondering if she needed a bath. The two Long Bow knights followed about fifteen feet behind—typically they paced at half that distance.

When the queen walked around the corner, two Long Bows who were crouched against the wall, stood, and approached her.

She turned to the knights following her. "Your replacements are here. Thank you. See you tomorrow."

"Yes, my queen."

They nodded at the two Long Bow guards and walked away.

She slowly turned to the two new knights.

"Good afternoon gentlemen. I think I will take a nap."

With a quick response the tall knight said, "Queen Althea. Please forgive me, but we have been asked to escort you to the location where Oscar and Kendrick have the twins."

She straightened her back and lifted her head—a smile graced her face.

"How wonderful! How are the twins? Where did you find them? Do you have the kidnappers in custody?"

"Oscar asked us to escort you to them."

That seems an odd request from Oscar. "Why do I need to go there?" she asked.

"One of the girls is injured, and the other twin is acting irrational. Oscar thought you might be a calming presence—they like you." The knight paused, then added, "If you ask me, Oscar is just afraid to move them in this condition."

Something in his story was making her uncomfortable, or was it the walk and the fear of another disagreeable eating episode? She placed her mouth in her elbow trying to hide a burp. She was hungry and weak from three days of illness.

"I will get my coat. Have you been here long?" Althea asked.

"No, we just arrived. We have a horse waiting for you, my queen."

She considered his explanation. Troubled, it repeated like the slow drumbeat of a death-march. A drumbeat that continued to haunt hours after the drum was silent. Boom. You might be a calming presence. Boom. He did not respond to my Where-are-they question. Boom. Oscar is afraid. Boom. Why not Samantha their mother? Boom.

They were half way down the back stairwell when she realized they had a horse waiting. She knew Oscar would have instructed one of them to escort her and one to get the horse to save time. The two Long Bows were waiting crouched in the hallway—not urgently looking for her. And she was certain Oscar would have found a clever way to bring the girls home. He was not one to ask or need help with his responsibilities.

She abruptly spun to question them, only to find one escort holding a dagger.

"Before you scream, remember we have the twins. If we do not arrive at the meeting spot by sunset tomorrow, they will be killed," said the other outlaw.

She continued down the stairs and slowed her pace hoping someone would see her. Upon exiting the castle two more knights and three horses were waiting. The smell of smoke saturated the air—on a Sunday, most families would be home for lunch. The younger rogue knight twisted in the saddle and stared at Althea. The older knight had faced his horse toward the door.

16

Althea noticed his small penetrating eyes, one brown and one white—returning to her every few seconds. Like her stepfather he was a drinking man with a large puffy nose accented with numerous small red veins. Long black hair framed his large round face. And his big shoulders topped a square body.

His large hands pointed to the horses. "Your horse is in the middle. Don't try to be heroic. Your foolishness only insures the twins' deaths. We could simply ride away and the girls' lives would be taken. Understood?" the confident leader asked.

"I understand!"

The horses' hooves clapped the cobblestone streets as they calmly rode toward the front gate. Occasionally, one of the horses would whinny, nicker, or snort. Church had been over for an hour. Not a single person roamed the streets. She saw multiple fresh scrapes on the cobblestones, and wondered if the twins had been kidnapped there.

I am in trouble. Althea twirled and toyed with the reins. She would not be missed until tomorrow when the maid picked up her uneaten dinner, or the sergeant took his tour of guarding. Althea felt helpless and alone—no one knew of her fate.

But what was that? Althea's heart beat as if it might jump out of her chest. There, on the next street over standing in a second floor window was an elderly woman waving to her. Althea made eye contact and acknowledged the woman with a nod.

* * *

Mid-afternoon, Kendrick slapped the reins from side to side and leaned over the horse's mane. At the last possible moment, he rose in the saddle and tugged the running horse to a stop. He bit his lower lip before clearing his throat.

"Kendrick, what did you find?" Oscar asked.

"The trail splits at the beginning of Dragon's Back," Kendrick replied. He rubbed the back of his neck. "And, they have picked up more men."

"Flaming dragons," Oscar whispered.

"I am not from around here. What is the Dragon's back?" asked a Long Bow.

"Dragon's Back is an outcropping of thousands of slate slabs pressed together standing on edge. It takes a day to ride its length and it is more than three miles wide. Some locations are higher than most two-story barns. Traversing it is a major obstacle," Oscar replied. He ran his fingers through his hair, and then rubbed his chin with his palm.

"We will have to go around the edges," Oscar continued. "Kendrick, take these four men with you and stay together. This could be a trap planned by the kidnappers to deal with a smaller chase group."

"Yes sir, Captain Oscar." He watched Kendrick's deliberate eye contact, and the forced smile. He knew it continued to irritate Kendrick calling his father Captain Oscar in public and on duty.

"Reginald, you are with me. Take this knife. If we get into a fight, you watch our rear for the enemy."

"Yes, sir."

He understood Reginald's motivation, but wished he had stayed home; Oscar worried he might have to fight the kidnappers and protect Reginald at the same time.

"Let us get started," Oscar ordered. He watched Kendrick and the four Long Bows until they turned the corner of Dragon's Back.

His sixth sense tingled. Something about this chase was wrong.

* * *

The quarter moon created dark shadows along the dense forested trail. Its frugal glimmer forced Kendrick to focus on the dimly lit path. After the third branch had smacked him in the face, Kendrick decided it was too dark to continue riding.

"We will make camp here tonight." He pointed at a couple of Long Bows and said, "You two gather some firewood. The rest of us need to find food."

Kendrick returned with roots and berries. Ten minutes later, two knights returned with a rabbit. While the food cooked, the young Long Bow knights told tales of their first adventure with Oscar. Kendrick was constantly being reminded of his father's greatness.

After eating, the stories continued until each of the knights had dozed off.

Suddenly the eerie howl of a wolf pierced the night waking them. Kendrick's father feared the black wolf more than any battle. The Long Bows' murmured uneasily. He did not turn to face them, because he was afraid they might see his fear.

"Each of us will take a two hour watch. I'll go first. Whoever is on watch at dawn, wake the rest of us," Kendrick said.

Kendrick intentionally walked twenty paces outside the camp's perimeter where the light of the campfire would not interfere with his night vision. Stopping frequently to study the dark, he hoped nothing was staring back.

On his third pass around the camp, in the clearing—two gold eyes stared at him. The animal's fur glistened in the limited moonlight. He guessed the wolf was seventy-yards away. He slowly pulled an arrow from the quiver and carefully loaded it in the bow.

Unexpectedly, something moved out of the dark void of the trees behind the wolf. To his surprise, an adolescent child wearing a flat brimmed monk's hat approached the wolf. Kendrick preparing to protect the child, quickly raised his bow, and paused to confirm the strange event. The child pointed, and the wolf followed into the darkness. Kendrick blinked several times, and then rubbed his eyes. Best to keep this to myself for now. They will not believe me anyway. He had thoughts and worried that the knights lacked confidence in him; that they followed orders because he was Oscar's son or maybe because he was the Queen's consort.

* * *

The sky began its circadian transformation. The fresh sunrise battled against the tired night sky for control of the day.

Kendrick was returning with an armful of firewood when he observed the watch knight wake two Long Bows. The three men frantically called out for Samuel and Kendrick.

"I am over here," Kendrick shouted.

"Have you seen Samuel?"

Kendrick ran to the campsite. "No. He was here when I left for firewood. Is he hunting for food? Maybe he is gathering firewood?"

Kendrick saw Samuel's bow, arrows, knife, and sword on the ground; and he knew it was required for a Long Bow to take his weapons everywhere.

"Each of us will take an area and look for Samuel." Kendrick placed the firewood next to the fire and assigned areas for searching.

He had the most difficult search. Most of the surface was rock with only a few small, scattered dirt patches. After a few minutes Kendrick found a small furrow of displaced dirt that continued on to the adjoining rock leaving a fresh dirt trail. Kneeling down to inspect the dirt he found the small rut's edges were crisp and not aged by wind or rain.

Tracking the random drag marks, he found an occasional partial boot print in the dirt patches. He crested a knoll. Ahead, Kendrick saw a man lying face down with his head awkwardly hanging over the edge of the large rock. He called out to Samuel but received no response. When he arrived at the body, there was a crimson pool below Samuel's head.

"Come quickly, I found Samuel!" Kendrick yelled.

Kendrick turned the body on his back. A burning acidy taste swelled up in his throat and he had to swallow several times to extinguish the pain. It was difficult to stop looking—his mind struggling with the thoughts of how awful to die from a slashed throat. Focus. Kendrick, focus. He swiped a sample from the pool then rubbed it between his thumb and forefinger.

The enemy was close.

Kendrick stood. His eyes alternating between squinting and staring as the morning's long dark shadows made examining the woods challenging. But, every snap, wisp, flutter, or irregularity was checked.

The knight on watch pulled a bloody piece of cloth from Samuel's mouth and laid it over the gash in the neck. "He was a good friend, and about to be a father." Quickly he turned away, bent over, his body shuddered several times.

Another knight wiped tears from his eyes.

Kendrick felt a lump in his throat as he checked the forest for kidnappers. A few moments later his heart felt like it would leap from his body. He saw movement in the trees. He had pulled an arrow from his quiver before he determined it was a large bird landing.

The other knights stared at Kendrick.

"What are you doing?" a knight asked.

"When I arrived the blood pool was still expanding and the warm blood was slick. Cooling blood is tacky. The kidnappers were here within the last ten minutes," Kendrick replied. The Long Bows exchanged glances, then as if conducted, the three knights looked to Kendrick. He knew they looked for guidance.

There was an unnerving silence. Kendrick felt they were being watched. "We need to cover Samuel. Use some of those big slabs," Kendrick said while continuing to scan the forest.

For fifteen minutes, the Long bows were sweating while lifting and hauling the heavy stone slabs from the Dragon's Back and placing them over Samuel's body.

Their hats removed, heads bowed, a Long Bow said a prayer.

"Amen."

Kendrick lifted his head. He felt something—a presence. Could the angels have come for Samuel's soul? No, this feeling was haunting. Maybe it was the wolf and the child? No, he would feel curiosity.

Kendrick wished he could allow extra time to grieve, but their immediate duty was to the queen's family. Every minute the kidnappers were progressing ahead. He walked toward the camp and nervously bit the inside of his cheek while thinking about an eminent encounter with the kidnappers. The others solemnly followed, gathered their belongings, then mounted their horses to continue along the side of Dragon's Back.

"Do you feel like we are not alone?" one knight asked.

"Yes. It's unsettling," another replied.

Kendrick nodded his head in silence remembering his father's warning to be careful about falling into a trap. He must be more diligent in protecting the rest of his men.

Traveling was difficult. Riding the horses, they had to duck under branches and fall back to keep from being slapped by a whipping limb. Or, they had to concentrate on placing their feet on stable ground when walking the horse. The terrain was gradually separating the group.

Kendrick estimated they had travelled about two miles when he looked behind and saw the group had suddenly become four individual riders.

Kendrick's thoughts boiled over as he remembered Father advised traveling as a group. He decided to close ranks by waiting for the other knights to catch up.

Shiiooft.

A tingling sensation darted up his spine. He shivered.

It was the sound Kendrick knew too well. He glanced back to see the last Long Bow of their small caravan clinching an arrow stuck in his right lung.

"Take cover!" Kendrick shouted, diving behind an outcropping of rock slabs. He checked on the two Long Bows—one was twenty yards away and hid behind a large tree trunk, and the other was about thirty-five yards away and behind a fallen tree.

Kendrick rolled over to spy around the edge of the outcropping. An enemy archer was taking aim from behind and above the knights. With scarce time to stop the archer before he struck one of his fellow knights, Kendrick released the arrow, striking the enemy below the ribs. The archer lost his balance and plunged head first to the ground between the two Long Bows. The startled knights acknowledged their thanks with a nod.

Kendrick rolled onto his stomach to assess the situation. There were three piles of rocks in the meadow—only two piles useful as cover in their attack, the third was on the far edge of the meadow.

Kendrick thought about the strategy of using the two rock piles. He turned to the two knights prepared to set his plan in motion when he saw two new archers on the cliff with bows drawn above the knights. Before Kendrick could warn them, the last two Long Bows were dead. Kendrick's heart pounded in his chest as he looked to see if archers were above him. Kendrick got up on one knee and released his arrow striking the nearest archer in the stomach. Instinctively he crouched and heard the arrow pass overhead. Kendrick's cover had become a liability. The archer across the meadow was not likely to miss him again. But if he stayed, he was exposed to the archer on the cliff with nowhere safe to take cover. Kendrick decided to risk his life on the archer across the meadow because he had slightly more time to spot a flying arrow. He concentrated and jumped through the uneven rocky ground toward the cliff's base while attempting to position another arrow—it was impossible.

Kendrick had another ten yards to the base when his hat was struck by the cliff archer's arrow. He stopped momentarily. Loading the arrow, flexing the string, he aimed, and released the arrow. It hit the cliff archer's leg.

A wolf's barking penetrated the chilled spring air and had startled the archer above giving Kendrick time to hide under the cliff's edge. His eyes focused on the timberline across the meadow. He was in the open hoping to determine the location of the archer by observing the flight of the arrows.

Suddenly, a man, with a bow and quiver, burst into the open meadow. After fifteen feet, the archer turned abruptly to shoot at something behind him. Before he could draw the bow, the same man was on his back screaming for his life. Then silence.

A terrible way to die; yet Kendrick hoped the wolf had had his fill and would not be interested in him. He needed to keep track of the wolf's location.

Examining the ground, a portion of the shadows was displayed between the trees, which revealed maybe two archers? He checked the arrow and moved away from the cliff's base searching for what he hoped was the last archer.

Peering into the mid-morning sun, and only for an instant, he could make out the distorted image of the archer partially blocking the sun. Kendrick shot on intuition. He heard a groan followed by a thud.

A shadow moved across Kendrick's face. Quickly he returned to the safety under the cliff, and prepared another arrow—only three left. He watched the ground for another archer, but the shadows did not change. He moved away from the cliff and prepared to defend himself.

After a minute, Kendrick turned his attention to the wolf. He was awestruck. Across the meadow, the panting wolf sat beside the child with the monk's hat.

Distant Illusions

The past six hours of hard riding, and the lack of food had made her tired and weak. Suddenly, the leader held up his hand and Althea felt a shot of energy as she pulled the reins. But not quick enough as the two horses collided and began to snort at one another. Lieutenant Cromwell shot a glare of disgust at Althea while straining to control his horse.

"It's the horse you provided. He is slow witted," Althea said.

"Humph," Charles grunted. "Get off the horse, we are going for a little walk."

One of the kidnappers gathered the reins. Althea noticed his sly smile as he walked off with the horses.

The setting sun cast an orange hue on the thick forest. The trail was lined with thick willows, thorny holly, and dense berry bushes. With her hands tied, she walked in the middle of her captures, at the same time looking for a place to escape. She would rather take a chance at being shot trying to escape then face a sure execution.

Cromwell was following a gradual bend in the path when a cave entrance appeared in the shadow of the trees. As they walked through the opening, she could feel the hot humidity. A minute inside the cave her foot struck a rock, she fell. Althea's toe throbbed and her palms burned. One of the soldiers grabbed the shoulder of her dress and lifted until her feet were slightly off the ground.

"Thank you," Althea said.

"Humph," came the reply. The man ushered her along the path controlling her with his hand above her elbow.

Following Charles' torch, the small parade continued deep into the cave.

The well-lit large room was a vivid contrast from the dark tunnel. Althea jerked her arm from the soldier's grip to shield her squinting eyes. She guessed thirty oil lamps, ten torches, and fifty candles illuminated the area. Cromwell walked her to a crate and offered his palm, pointing to sit. Cromwell signaled two men to watch her.

She estimated twenty men were opening and sorting the contents of several large wooden boxes—arrows, swords, weapon belts, and knives. Several stopped and stared at her. Although some of her Long Bows had longingly stared at her before—there was contempt on the faces of these men.

Cromwell shook hands with the leader, and both men placed their left hand on the traditional handshake. They talked for about three minutes and laughed. Cromwell looked to the ceiling and paused before he turned toward Althea. A wry smile graced his face momentarily.

"Men, this is the Queen of Manshire."

Cromwell leaned forward and loudly rushed his words, "Queen. Follow me."

The two soldiers followed her. Althea rubbed her nose trying to displace the smell of the hot mineral water coming from deeper in the cave. Perspiration collected at the small of her back. Darkness surrounded them outside the limits of Cromwell's torch—Althea tripped four times and managed to avoid the fifth. Cromwell entered with the torch and had to bend his head, neck, and shoulders. He looked distorted bent over. She smiled.

Off the main tunnel, a small ten-foot long passage led to a room with a cot, water bucket, and one burning candle. The ceiling was perhaps six inches above her head on the high side, and four inches on the low side. The smooth floor sloped gently across the twenty-foot square room.

"This is your new home," he said.

"For how long, may I ask?" Althea inquired.

"As long as it takes to negotiate the return of Saraton to its rightful king."

26

Althea was thankful for the dim light, which hid her efforts to control her stiffening muscles and widening eyes. But she could not hide the gasp.

The humid air made the room hot and sticky and a strange whistling noise filled the cave. Althea slowed her breathing in an attempt to reduce the retched sulfur smell. The nausea escalated.

Charles moved the torch near her and stared. Althea initially thought he was looking for an advantage from a display of weakness. But, she decided it was a ruse so he could stare at her bright blue eyes. "Good, you will do well here. Your determination will keep you alive."

"Who will I be negotiating with?" Althea asked. He had lied several times today, why would she trust his answers now? Still, she had to ask.

"You are the leverage to get Oscar and Quentin to return Saraton to Argo, the former and exiled king's son. You will not be negotiating."

A shudder ran up her back. Oscar and Quentin—negotiating? Oscar would be good at interrogation, But Quentin? He was not prepared to interrogate or negotiate—he was simply too young. And, why not Kendrick? She reasoned there was time to devise a plan and trick this Argo prince into talking with her.

"Where are my twin sisters?"

Cromwell untied her hands as he spoke. "They are probably under Oscar's protection. Their kidnapping was a ruse to get Oscar and Kendrick out of the castle—allowing us to abduct you."

Her stomach discomfort was diminishing. Good. Now I can focus on my escape without worrying about my sisters.

Cromwell squatted. Althea assumed he felt more powerful with his head and neck aligned.

"A few rules for you to know. First, Kendrick is being followed. Any escape attempt by you will result in his death. Second, you will receive one meal each afternoon. Third, these guards outside the entrance to this room are two of several assigned to you. They have instructions to stop you at all costs—which might include your death. We merely need Oscar and Quentin to think you are alive." Charles lit another candle. "These candles last about nine hours. Use them wisely." He walked out of the room.

Nausea returned as she thought about Kendrick's fate.

Althea evaluated her new home. The ceiling, floor, and walls were a slate color with silver streaks—too much darkness for two little candles. A narrow passageway in the opposite corner of the large room connected to a smaller eight by fifteen oval room.

She walked along holding the candle near the walls.

Althea believed the colossal underground rock was a complex combination of various sized tubes as the large room had six holes of less than one-foot diameter, and the oval room had three holes, two small and one large.

The oval room scared her—was that ghosts she heard inside? I hope we are not trespassing on sacred burial grounds.

* * *

With an arrow in his bow, Kendrick moved slowly over the rocky surface quickly surveying the area, and prepared for another enemy archer. After three minutes he sat on a fallen tree, exhausted and shaking.

He was alone.

He had failed.

Leaning the bow against the tree, he stared at nothing in the meadow. Tears rolled down his cheeks. What have I done? All my men are dead. He knelt, interlaced his fingers, and prayed. Lord, please give me the strength to accept my failure and the knowledge of why these brave men had to die. I humbly ask that you are watching over Father and keeping him safe from harm— enough men have died today. I pray that we find the twins alive and healthy. Amen.

He stood, continued to stare at the ground, and placed his hands on the back of his head. He paced aimlessly around the rocks, bushes, and stumps for several minutes.

Pebbles crunching under foot caught his attention. He glanced in the direction of the slowly approaching sound that reminded him of the gravel in the stables. Kendrick reached for his long bow and winced after realizing the weapon was twenty-five yards away.

Walking quickly, he was less than halfway there, when a black wolf leaped in front of him. He stopped, jerked to catch his balance, and then stood still. His eyes were wide as he moved them to each side looking for a weapon. Kendrick couldn't find anything nearby to use defensively. His hands shook as he thought about having to fight the wolf with only the knife in his belt and left boot. Maybe he could thrust a few arrows from his quiver into the wolf's chest...

The wolf was not growling, but she was frightening. Oscar had taught Kendrick to avoid eye contact with wild animals, but he could not resist staring. Her large head connected atop the powerful front shoulders. The wolf was about a foot taller than the grey wolves Kendrick had encountered over the years.

More pebbles crunching caught Kendrick's attention, but he dare not move. Could it be another wolf?

He heard two thumps like a stick thrusting at a rock.

"Exeter. Come," came the deep voice from behind him.

Kendrick followed the wolf's gentle scamper over a few bushes where sat a small man wearing a monk's hat.

"She will not hurt you. Please feel free to move," the man said while gesturing for Kendrick to sit on a nearby rock. "My name is Bernard. And you are?"

The small man was about four and a half feet tall. His weathered face was revealed as he removed the monk's hat, wiping the sweat from his forehead. His eyes sparkled with confidence.

Kendrick's tense arms and legs relaxed somewhat. He swallowed a couple times to wet his dry throat.

"Kendrick from Manshire, Sir."

"Kendrick, meet Exeter. I have raised her from a puppy. You see. She is very calm," he said. Bernard's hand rubbed along the wolf's back. "She likes you. You must have a good heart. Please, come and sit with me."

Kendrick slowly moved toward his bow. He could see it leaning against the fallen tree.

Exeter stood.

"Leave the bow. There is a nice rock over here—just for you."

"Where are you from?" Kendrick asked, his attention alternating between the rocky, uneven ground, and the wolf.

Bernard stretched his arms and twisted at the hip. "I am from—here."

"You live in this forest?" Kendrick sat on the rock crossing his arms to hide his shaking hands.

"Yes. But, not from my own choosing. Why are you here?"

Kendrick glanced at his bow. His eyes looked to the ground as he rubbed the stubble on his chin.

"We are...I am searching for...kidnapped twins from...Manshire castle." His mind churned with thoughts that his mistakes had gotten four men killed, his soft voice tapering to a whisper. "You said not from your choosing," Kendrick continued. He raised his head to see Bernard leaning forward toward him, listening intently.

"The short version is my brother had the guards leave me in the forest when I was about fourteen. He was thirteen and wanted to insure there were no rivals challenging his ascension to the throne."

"You are a...prince?"

"By birth. The only way."

Kendrick's thoughts of Althea, the adopted princess, flashed across his mind. "What country?"

"My father was the king of Saraton until he was exiled," Bernard said.

Kendrick's eyes widened. He thought, Saraton royalty, should I be careful with what I say? He could be a spy. "Um, How did you, uh, survive?" Bernard's head tilted slightly. He paused momentarily.

"For three years, the step queen had food sent to me until she was caught by my brother," Bernard said.

"Caught? What happened?"

"My brother had her imprisoned, more like confined, for treason."

Kendrick noticed his hands were not shaking and rested them on his knees.

"How is she?" Kendrick wished he had not asked.

"Last I heard, she survived a year before escaping," Bernard said. "Now there is just my brother and me."

Exeter lifted her head and sniffed the air.

"Someone is coming. We must hide," Bernard said.

Kendrick examined the ground to the bow and the best path required him to run around three boulders and four bushes. He decided there was not time to collect the bow and hide.

"No time for that now," Bernard said. "Come quickly we must disappear!"

Not wanting to give up too quickly, Kendrick re-examined the path and whispered, "flaming dragons." Thinking he might need to protect Bernard, he turned to follow Bernard and Exeter into the forest. The wolf hurdled over anything in her path, stopping occasionally to check on Bernard—who had to run around everything in his path. Kendrick followed Bernard until he remembered Exeter protected Bernard.

He dove into the open center of a thicket of berry bushes. Bernard and Exeter were no longer in sight. How did they disappear so quickly? Kendrick knelt and peered through the bushes, deadfall, and branches.

Kendrick was surprised. From the bits and pieces he could see, the men looked like Long Bows. Recalling the kidnappers were dressed as Long Bows; he sat on the ground, his palms sweating, his shoulders tightening. With eyes closed, he lowered his head to concentrate on the sounds. He had to develop a scheme to retrieve his bow and horse—this plan would have to be executed at night.

Kendrick wondered how long it would take them to discover the dead bodies scattered under the cliff, and the horses that had wandered off into the forest across the meadow. Would they start searching for survivors? Was his bow still safely hidden amongst the branches? Could he make a bow with the available materials?

The day had been one difficult struggle after another. Exhaustion jumbled his thoughts. He resisted the urge to sleep until exhaustion finally crushed his will.

He napped.

Moments later, his eyes popped open. He was staring at the ground shivering, wondering if he had actually cried out during the nightmare when the archer's arrow struck his chest.

Could it be he heard children's voices? He raised his head slowly. Could the kidnappers be a mere seventy yards away?

* * *

Althea lit another candle then attempted a nap—still tossing and turning for what seemed to be an hour by the burn of the candle, and then sat up on the edge of the cot. She stared at the white veins in the grey floor, her hands cradling her face, her elbows resting on her knees. Beads of sweat occasionally dripped off her nose. She looked through the entry passage. One of the guards waved to her.

Events were untangling, and although they made her angry, she appreciated their clever tactical design. Cromwell was a good soldier but could not have planned the twins kidnapping to remove the major threats of Oscar and Kendrick, for access to the real target—me. But Argo— must be a patient planner. The soldiers had near perfect Long Bow clothing, and knew where they needed to go. And, if that was true, Argo had probably thought about the negotiations and had plotted how to best Oscar and Quentin. Argo must have spies in Manshire. And that means my father-in-law and stepbrother must be walking into a trap.

She brushed her hair with her fingers, stood, then paced the room recalling the events that had led her to this predicament. Passing the oval room she heard faint voices from the two-foot hole near the floor of her prison. The faint conversation caught her attention.

"... more target practice—men in camp—ready in two months—return in two weeks—be prepared for skills test—she has no purpose after the..."

A muffled sound like a large box being pulled across a floor replaced the voices. A minute later, from behind she heard the shuffle of boots coming down the passage.

* * *

Kendrick's mind was full of the events that had transpired the past two days including the kidnapped twins and his own guilt for losing four men. He shook his head—I have to concentrate on the twins rescue.

Observing the men twenty-yards from his bow, he was thankful it blended in with branches of the fallen tree. There were several single or small patches of short berry bushes scattered between him and his bow. He had to leave the thicket through the back hedge to avoid detection, and though the course he had planned was far from direct, it would place him near his bow. Kendrick had to crawl to stay below the enemy's sight line.

The slightest noise, or puff of dirt, could bring him unwanted attention. Slowly he pushed through the rear of the thicket. Every few inches his head jerked back and a spot of blood oozed from the new scratch. He grimaced when the branches poked into his pant legs.

Hunched over, Kendrick had escaped the thicket. He wiped the blood from his face with his fingers, and then accessed the condition of his pants—a few small random tears that would not rip or create a problem during the rescue. He squatted behind the bushes listening for footsteps. A few moments later he began his careful crawl toward the first patch of bushes. The pine needles and small stones poked and scratched his knees. Small branches were carefully lifted from the path and placed to the side to prevent their snap from disclosing his location.

Sweat formed on his forehead and hands.

Kendrick could only see one rogue knight watching the playing twins. After a few minutes, Elsa suddenly yelled. Kendrick halted, raised his head, and turned an ear toward the noise. He was exposed, just three feet from his first hiding spot. He remained still to avoid attracting any attention, fighting an instinct to rush the camp, grab his bow, and start shooting. He had to be mindful of the girls' safety.

Erma screamed. He assumed the twins had discovered one of the dead archers.

The twins' guard gestured toward some soldiers who came running. They gathered near an archer, then walked toward the cliff. Kendrick heard their voices but could not make out the words.

A man on a white horse with grey spots, appeared from the forest on the west side of the meadow.

Kendrick recognized the quiver, and the old comfortable saddle.

It was Father.

* * *

Althea quickly turned from the hole, and then forced herself to slowly walk with her hands behind her back. She had taken four steps when Cromwell entered the room and placed a chair near the entrance.

"Pacing?" Cromwell asked.

"Cannot sleep and this calms me," Althea replied.

"Good. I will be gone for a short while. The guards have instructions to keep you alive, but should you try to escape, their orders are to tie you to that chair." The wooden legs appeared to be shorter than most chairs, and the shredded seat looked like it might collapse at any moment.

She stared at the chair for a few moments, then caught Cromwell's sly smile.

"Please, let me negotiate with Argo."

"I will ask, but expect a 'no'. And it is King Argo."

She ignored his correction. "You could just take me there."

"Sorry. I have several stops to make before meeting with Argo. I cannot risk you escaping, or discovering Argo's plan. Be good and I will give you extra candles."

"Sure," Althea replied, wondering if she could now thwart Argo's plans and escape. She listed her resources—the cot's wood, cot's webbing, water and bucket, one to three candles, a meal each day, the listening hole, her wits, her dress, and a dilapidated chair. The realization that the list was of no value re-enforced the proficiency Argo had put into her kidnapping.

* * *

The archer entered the cave's large open area and approached Cromwell. His clothes were dirty and smelled of sweat.

"Lieutenant, Cromwell, Sir."

"Yes."

"I wish to report success on our mission to eliminate the Long Bows in Kendrick's group, but we lost five archers in the raid."

"Five archers dead? What happened? I picked the perfect ambush point."

"Kendrick is an excellent marksman. Much better than we were informed."

Cromwell slowly stroked his chin with his palm—he was uncertain what King Argo would think about a successful mission that lost all warriors but one.

"I have to make several stops to review the other soldier camps. The king would want this information right away," Cromwell said.

"Before I forget, we also saw an unusual, actually strange, event," the soldier offered, pausing briefly to take in his surroundings.

Lieutenant Charles Cromwell's hands rested on his hips. His narrowed eyes focused on the soldier.

"Well?" Cromwell demanded.

"A wolf, controlled by a small man, attacked one of our men."

Charles had heard these strange rumors for a couple years. "Did he wear a monk's hat?"

"Yes. How did you know?"

"I saw this man and his wolf a while ago," Charles replied, not sure he wanted to tell Argo the news. "I need you to get this information to King Argo quickly. Can you deliver this vital news to our king?"

"Yes. I would be honored to be the messenger."

"Take some food with you and leave for Venela while there are still a few hours of light. Go straight to King Argo. You should be there in three to four days."

"Yes sir."

* * *

Kendrick was five feet outside the tree line when Elsa pointed, "Look Father, it's Kendrick, and he is bleeding."

"Yes he is," Reginald replied. A smile graced his face. He waved to Kendrick.

Oscar walked toward Kendrick and picked up Kendrick's bow leaning against the tree. Father and son walked quickly through the bushes and boulders, both focused on the rugged terrain. When their eyes met, Oscar noticed the facial scratches and blood streaks. It was cause for a momentary delay before he handed the bow to Kendrick and they shook hands. Oscar wanted to hug him, but did not want to embarrass him in front of his fellow Long Bows.

Oscar rubbed the palm of his hand on Kendrick's cheek. "Are you alright? Your face is bleeding." He looked around at the bodies. "So, what happened here?"

"I will be okay. The short version is—it started early when we discovered Samuel was removed from the camp. We found him after a few minutes with his throat cut." Kendrick's hands shook. "About two hours later we were ambushed. A rogue archer killed the last knight in the line. The other two knights and I found cover. Our backs w-were to the cliff when I-I rolled over an archer who was preparing to sh-shoot the two remaining Long Bows."

"It is okay. Be calm," Oscar whispered.

He knew if another knight had lost four knights in battle, Oscar would be interrogating the leader.

"I dispatched the archer on the cliff, assessed our position, and determined it was best to attack the archer across the meadow. That's when two more archers appeared on the cliff and shot two Long Bows. I was able to hit both rogue archers; one fell from the cliff, the other one only wounded. Hiding under the cliff for cover, the third archer's shadow told me danger was looming. When I jumped out, the archer was in the sun. I took a chance and was successful." He rubbed the back of his neck and looked at his boots, gestures that revealed Kendrick held something back. Oscar decided to discuss it when he could have a private meeting with Kendrick.

Though his son appeared low in spirits, Oscar was confident he would quickly put this tragedy in perspective. I wish you would take up another occupation. It is so hard to see you like this.

Two Long Bows moved the bodies of the dead men alongside each other and covered them with rocks and slate slabs. A tear ran down Kendrick's cheek when they prayed for the dead Long Bows.

"Mount up. We need to return Elma and Erma back to the castle," Oscar ordered.

New Friends

Quentin's attention was drawn to the squeaking oak floor. He watched as a bent grey haired woman slowly scanned the cathedral's interior from one side to the other—stopping when she saw the confessional. Her mannerisms told him she had not been here before. Running her fingers through her long grey hair seemed to resolve her intentions and dissipate her uncertainty.

The lady slowly limped to the confessional, slid the heavy curtain aside, looked around, stepped in, then closed the curtain.

Quentin entered the other confessional cubicle, slid the privacy door open, and asked, "How can I help you, my child?" He was immediately embarrassed—my child, had slipped out by habit. "I apologize for saying my child."

"Not to worry, I was flattered. Thank you," she replied.

"What is it you wish to confess?"

"Before I tell you, is our conversation a secret?"

"Yes. Only God, you, and I will know the contents of this confession."

"Good." She paused. "Because I am worried about being beaten, or worse. You know kidnapping goes on even today under our new queen."

Quentin was confident she was correct, but asked anyway, "Are you sure people are kidnapped today?"

"Yes!" she replied. Her loud response appeared to startle even her. "I better go. I could bring trouble upon me." Her voice quivered.

"Wait." Quentin tried to keep his voice calm. "I promise your confession is safe with me."

There was a lengthy silence. Quentin knew she was there because he had not heard the curtain slide open. "Let me help you."

"Okay," she whispered.

"I saw the queen leave with four other men. They were quietly riding toward the drawbridge. The queen looked into my eyes and nodded."

The admission surprised Quentin. He sat for a few moments trying to figure out what to say next.

The pause must have scared her—he heard the curtain rings slide across the rod. Quick, say something to stop her. "Wait. Why are you scared of this information being known by anyone else?" he whispered. The silence lasted forever.

The curtain scratched across the rod.

"The horseman behind the queen ran his finger across his throat and pointed at me."

"Do you have any relatives you could stay with for a while?" he asked.

"No, young man, there is just me—the second wife of an exiled king."

* * *

The day had turned dark and gloomy with heavy cloud cover. A misty rain soaked their clothes and Oscar was certain a storm this afternoon would assault them but again. It was another aspect of this rescue that was troubling to Oscar.

Erma rode with her father, and Elsa rode with Kendrick. Oscar rode ahead to check the trail, determined to finally have control of their safe return. Since leaving the castle, he had felt manipulated and uneasy. Reginald's story disturbed him because the kidnappers appeared to be unconcerned with the attention from the yelling and screaming during the abduction. And the final unsettling questions were—where had these child thieves gone and why had they left the girls by a campfire—how did they make their tracks vanish?

An hour into the ride, Oscar and a pair of Long Bows rapidly approached Kendrick and Reginald.

"What is happening?" Kendrick asked.

"The queen disappeared yesterday, and no one knows where she is," Oscar replied. "I am going to the castle to see what is happening." He turned to Kendrick—his eyes clear, shoulders back, and head up. These were traits Oscar admired in his son; not dwelling on the past, and learning from his mistakes. Oscar watched as Kendrick's determined, urgent expression melted into understanding that the best use of their skills required his son to care for the girls.

"I will escort the twins. Father, you go ahead to the castle."

"These two knights will ride with you. If you keep a good pace you can reach the castle by sunset." He pulled the reins to the right, kicked the horse's hips, and in an instant was riding away.

During the ride, Oscar analyzed the events of the past two days—noisy kidnapping, easy tracking, split trails, ambush of Kendrick's team, twins left at campfire, Kendrick the only survivor, and the queen's disappearance. How did these events connect?

Four hours later, he crossed the drawbridge. Oscar saw insecurity in the citizens' eyes—within seconds of dismounting the din of questions overwhelmed him. Repeatedly, clenching his jaw while quickly inhaling, preparing to answer, then relaxing his chin as he exhaled, heightened his frustration. The volume of questions made it impossible to answer and comfort the crowd. He raised his hands and the crowd went silent.

"I share your confusion and promise to inform you of the queen's status as soon as I can," Oscar said. An unnerving tingle shivered up his spine.

Oscar began his inquiry with the sergeant who was tasked with Althea's protection.

"How did this happen? And, where were you?" Oscar asked.

"Near as I can tell, she disappeared about an hour before I planned to relieve the guards on duty. The two guards said she dismissed them when their replacements arrived. We searched every room in the castle, barracks, and cathedral. We checked the stables and courtyards. And finally, every house and shop within the outer wall. If people were not home, we broke the door, and searched the house." The sergeant was about to speak when Oscar held up his hand.

"You were scheduled to replace the previous guard team, yes?"

"Yes."

"The guards mentioned they were relieved of duty," Oscar said. "Did the two guards recognize the replacements?"

"No."

Oscar toyed with the hair in his short beard.

"Anything unusual in the home search?"

"No sir."

"How many homes did you break into?"

"Maybe a dozen?"

"Have you accounted for all the occupants?"

"There are four people we still need to question."

"Follow-up with those four. It is a long shot, but we cannot afford to overlook any single clue."

Oscar also questioned the queen's chambermaid, the kitchen staff that delivered her meals, and the two guards. Each one's story was unique, but no one knew how or when the queen had vanished.

His jaw clinched as he paced. There were no clues. Flaming Dragons!

Angry Shadows

The nation of Cyphera, a large island with the western coastline a partial desert compared to the lush green eastern coast. A low mountain range formed a horseshoe from the middle of the western shores toward the north and down along the eastern farming area.

Venela was the largest city and capital of Cyphera. Located between the northern most edge of the mountain range and the shoreline, it was neither in the desert or lush green portion, and enjoyed the best of each area. Coffee, cotton, olives, and dates were the products of the western arid climate. Fruits, vegetables, nuts, and wine were produced in hundreds of these small eastern farms.

Outside of Venela was the palace of the exiled Saraton king and family. The king had died three years after skipping out of Saraton. Fourteen-year-old Prince Argo had been left to rule the displaced kingdom, as his eldest siblings had vanished.

The king had a profound influence on his younger son; Argo longed for the return to Saraton and all the pleasures of a royal lifestyle. Until that time, a frustrated Argo had portions of the old converted winery remodeled to match the image Father had rooted in his mind. Fine pewter dishes, gold trimmed goblets, and silver utensils adorned the linen place setting surrounded by fresh fruit, vegetables, bread, and roasted ham shank.

Although his life was safe and easy, he wanted the life of his father—servants, personal cook, tailored clothes, several castles, and ultimate power.

The personal valet waited for Argo to finish lunch before approaching.

"Sire, an archer sent by Lieutenant Cromwell has arrived with a message."

"Bring him forward." Argo walked to the throne, drew a deep breath, and slowly exhaled.

The archer entered the throne room with his head bowed, careful not to look into Argo's eyes. Three paces from the throne the two guards stepped toward the archer. He stopped and knelt, waiting for Argo to acknowledge him.

"What message do you bring from the lieutenant?"

Staring at the floor, the archer said, "We successfully ambushed the Manshire Long Bows, killing all but the queen's husband, as you instructed."

A smile graced Argo's face, but for a moment. He sensed a hesitation and the archer's head bowed a little further.

"What is it that you are not telling me?"

"My king, I am the only survivor." He quickly added, "Kendrick is an excellent marksmen."

Argo stood and paced the edge of the throne platform. "Is there anything else, you have to report?" he said. There was a hint of anger in his voice, but he did not care how the messenger perceived his inquiry.

"Yes, my king." The archer's voice trembled. "There was a black wolf controlled by a short man, helping Kendrick. The wolf attacked one of our soldiers."

The rumors are true. "Is there more to the message?"

"No."

"Did you attempt to dispatch the small man, or the wolf?"

"No your grace. Kendrick eliminated everyone. I considered it my duty to deliver this message as soon as possible."

The unmistakable ring of a sword yanked from a scabbard surprised the archer. He looked up to see Argo's red face. It was too late. A flash of light reflected off the blade as Argo plunged it into the archer's heart.

"Coward, you should have destroyed the small man," Argo whispered.

* * *

Kendrick wandered through the market alone. His thoughts, an assortment of disjointed events—abducted twins, abandonment, ambush, Althea's disappearance, and a void of information created an uncontrollable whirlpool sensation within his brain. He was unable to sort or link the events for analyzing, and every beat of his aching heart desperately wanted action that would fill the void. The past three days appeared to be an unfortunate coincidence of bad luck.

Victor, the new market sheriff, was easy to spot because he was five inches taller than the crowd. In his black tunic he crossed through the sea of patrons toward Kendrick. Victor approached with his signature smile and extended his hand. Kendrick found comfort in his strong grip.

Eighteen months ago, happenstance had brought them together at the Blacksmith, as their horses had needed a shoe replaced. He recalled the conversation flowed with the ease of smooth water in a flat river.

"Where do you live?" Kendrick asked.

"I am looking for a new home and job—lived up north until five months ago." Victor replied.

The rhythm of the blacksmith's hammer skipped a beat.

Kendrick saw the quiver hanging on the saddle and the bow leaning against a hay bale.

"Nice bow. It looks like you take good care of it."

"It was my father's. He gave it to me about seven years ago." Victor handed the bow to Kendrick.

Kendrick positioned the bow and pulled the string twice. "Good action. It is a nice bow." He handed it back to Victor. "I would be happy to show you some good hunting areas. At least you will not go hungry."

Victor had mirrored Kendrick's posture.

"So, you are looking for a job?" Kendrick asked.

"Yes. Do you know anyone needing a strong laborer?" Victor leaned forward and rubbed his hands together.

Kendrick wished his arms had not instinctively folded. He thought it best to leave them crossed, rather than reveal his reluctance. He licked his lips before nervously saying, "I might know of an opportunity." He hesitated a few seconds. "This evening, drop by the barracks, so I can get you a temporary bunk. Meet me here tomorrow morning and I will show you a few places to hunt and fish."

"Your horse is finished," said the blacksmith to Victor.

"What do I owe you?" Victor asked.

Behind Victor, Kendrick caught the blacksmith's attention by tapping his chest three times.

"You are so lucky, as my five hundredth customer, it is free."

Victor turned to Kendrick. "Thank you, that is very kind of you." He picked up his bow and guided his horse through the shop doors. "See you later at the barracks."

Kendrick waived.

A few minutes passed as the blacksmith hummed a song while shoeing Kendrick's horse.

"Nice guy," Kendrick said.

"Strange though, the shoe looked as if it had been pried from the hoof. The dirt had been flattened in a couple spots. And I think the red mud was from south of here," said the blacksmith.

Kendrick did not think too much about the flat spots or the red mud. Victor might have been in the south looking for work, and had had to pry off a loose shoe.

* * *

Kendrick enjoyed the colorful morning, trimmed with bright orange and pink—chance of rain.

Victor rode up and dismounted. His smile revealed a perfect set of white teeth. They shook hands.

"Thanks for arranging the barrack's bunk. The captain said I could stay for a few weeks."

"Are you ready for the best hunting in Manshire?"

"Sure."

For an hour their conversation consisted of short bursts prompted by observations and separated by silence. Yesterday's smooth river was drying up.

"When the road splits in a mile, go left. At the stone marker, we will be at the greatest hare field in Manshire," Kendrick said.

New vines nearly covered the mound of apple-sized rocks at the road's edge. Kendrick tugged the reins, dismounted, and drew his knife to cut the vines back. The cuttings were tossed into the nearby foliage.

"Were you going to let me wander past the marker?" Victor said, revealing his contagious smile. He dismounted, shouldered his quiver, and gathered the bow. Victor drew an arrow. Kendrick raised his eyebrows—the smooth, quick motion reminded him of Father.

Fifteen yards into the field, three rabbits dashed from behind a bush—two arrows struck the bucks instantly. A third arrow immediately found the doe. Kendrick, a few steps from Victor, shook his head, "That was impressive. Where did you learn to hunt like that?"

"The duke's kitchen." Victor's grin revealed his tease.

"Kitchen?" Kendrick smiled.

"My father was the head cook for Duke Earl Brandt. The duke loved to party—so Father was not home much. I was responsible to gather food for my mother and sister when I was old enough to cast a hook and set traps. A year later, Father taught me to hunt with a bow. We met twice a week at the kitchen's scrap heap—where he taught me to shoot rats between meal preparations."

"How does your family gather food without you?"

"They died from lung fever." Victor said.

"Sorry, I did not know."

"I miss them, especially my younger sister. Her battle was difficult to accept. Her young body struggling to breathe between coughing spells."

Kendrick knew Victor's pain. He wiped a tear from his eye as memories of his mother's disease flooded his mind. Still he was able to enjoy the day with Victor, and discovered they had a lot in common—he also had to provide food for family, a father not being home, bow training, and a family illness. Kendrick wanted to help Victor. The previous evening, Father had answered his job inquiry: "Proxmire will be entering the Long Bows soon and you will need to find a new sheriff soon," he had said.

Kendrick took a deep breath then exhaled slowly. "I need someone to provide safety and protection in the market."

Victor's smile expanded. "What does the job require?"

"Mostly, catching thieves and stopping fights among the customers."

"I can do that."

* * *

Kendrick's thoughts returned to the present. He was happy to see Victor. Typically they shook hands, but Kendrick hugged Victor.

"Ah...Yes," Victor said. His voice had a higher pitch. Then he placed a fist over his lips and cleared his throat a couple times. "Good to see you my friend. I have heard the rumors of your unfortunate adventures. Can I be of service to you?" Victor asked. A few seconds passed before Victor's smile returned.

"Yes my friend. I need to talk with someone that can help me examine the strange events of the last three days."

"The market is full of rumors, speculation, and fear. I have heard that Queen Althea slipped away in the night because she was afraid of what her natural mother would say about the twins' kidnapping. There is talk that she cannot take the pressure, and has returned to the family farm. Most people scoff at these prophecies. The most troublesome conversations are about the fear of the unknown—what will happen to their lives if the queen does not return soon."

"Have you heard anything unusual that has an element of possibility?" Kendrick asked.

Victor rubbed his chin with his thumb and first finger.

"An old lady claimed to have seen the queen willfully riding with four men on Sunday afternoon. Standing in front of a cart and interrupting sales, the merchant told her to confess to a priest. I escorted her to the edge of the market area. She thanked me, then walked away toward the village."

"Do you know where she lives?"

"No. I did not think to ask. I thought she was mindless."

"Do you know what she looks like? Would you recognize her again?"

"Sure...sure." Victor eagerly replied. "But I do not know where she lives."

Finally, a clue, but no progress—someone we cannot find who might know something.

Drunken Decisions

Lieutenant Charles Cromwell rode alone to camp number two. He had taken this route five times collecting information, analyzing troop progress, watching training sessions, and reporting to King Argo—a task that brought sweat to his forehead and shaking to his hands, although in the remote areas of the former Saraton, he worried about thieves. Still between Argo and the thieves, if he could choose, he would rather deal with the thieves.

Arriving at the second camp, the hundred soldiers stationed there were nowhere to be found. Cromwell worried that the men had been discovered by Manshire patrols and jailed, or worse.

He checked his bearings. He was between the bald topped mountains and a mile north of Snow Lake. He couldn't be more than a few hundred yards from the training site. This location had been selected because the wider distance between the trees helped the warriors train to dodge arrows in battle.

The forested area was unnervingly quiet as the natural sounds were absent.

Cromwell dismounted, dropped the reins, and drew an arrow. Stalking the edge of the petite clearing he wondered what could have happened to his men. In ten minutes he had completed the loop. Relieving the tension on the bow only made him more anxious.

The sounds of birds chirping had returned. Some unusual bush rustling came from behind.

Suddenly, hundreds of arrows were flying. He turned to run away from them, only to discover that arrows flew from every direction, but not at him. He squatted, placed his hands over his head, and hoped he survived the ambush. Now he knew how the

Manshire posse felt that had been ambushed at Dragon's Back. It must be a large Manshire Long Bow squadron to draw so many arrows and guard the Saraton group.

Laughter came from the forest. The deep authoritative voice of the Second Lieutenant called out to Cromwell. "It is okay lieutenant. I hope you appreciate our demonstration."

Cromwell had been unnerved looking for the warriors. The burst of arrows made him think he might die. But he could not let his tension rob the warriors of their pride. He crossed his arms and nodded his head.

"It was quite impressive. King Argo will be happy to hear of your skills," Cromwell said.

"Yes, I will." The familiar high-pitched, feminine voice of Argo surprised Cromwell. "Second Lieutenant, the demonstration was impressive."

He bowed. "My king, it is good to see you. I have much good news to report."

Cromwell studied his king for a few brief moments and wondered how a physically weak man like Argo could become so powerful.

"Second Lieutenant, carry-on," Argo said. "Charles, we need to talk—over here." He pointed to a couple logs on the edge of the clearing.

After they had sat, the king's dozen guards formed a large circle around them.

"First, how is the Manshire queen? Athena is it?"

"Althea," Cromwell replied, instantly wishing he had let it go uncorrected. "Sorry, my king, it is a bad habit."

"Do I have to worry about you growing fond of this, Althea?"

Cromwell hoped the short pause did not incriminate him. "It is not a problem." He noticed Argo raise an eyebrow.

"I can depend on you to execute the plan when needed?"

"Yes, my king. I have no affection for her," Cromwell said, thinking he had just lied to Argo. If caught, that was an act that could shorten his life.

"How much longer before the troops are ready?"

"I can provide a better assessment after I visit the seven Cyphera locations. So far, group one needs another three weeks. Group two, as you have witnessed is ready. And from my last tour, group six and eight are about ready. I am guessing that in four weeks every camp will be ready. Then we will need two weeks to get them in position."

"I hope Howard is sure the priest Prince Quentin is next in line for the throne. We have been fortunate to meet him, but if he is wrong we will all be executed. I wish to add a contingency plan to our invasion. If we fail, I want Howard the Librarian, Oscar, Kendrick, Althea, and Quentin to be assassinated. Regardless of the outcome of our invasion, Manshire will be destroyed."

"Yes, my king, it will be done," Cromwell replied.

"Excellent. Is the boat ready?"

"If the seven camps on Cyphera are near ready as we suspect. I will make the final arrangements for the boat to transport them to Saraton."

Argo stood and looked down at Cromwell. "One last task—Bernard is alive. Send a team out to kill him, and that wolf. Do not fail me. Bernard can unravel our plans." Argo's rage was near explosion. Last time Cromwell witnessed this anger, a man lost his hand for stealing one of Argo's apples.

Instantly Argo's tense muscles softened and his voice's congenial tone had returned.

"I want to commend you for your clever suggestion of training most of the troops in Cyphera and arranging the boat to transfer the militia to Saraton." Argo paced slowly for about a minute, then added, "You did well Charles, my good friend. Let us hope for continued good fortune." Argo paused, then whispered, "We are running out of money."

He thought of the good fortune that had blessed Argo the past eleven months and how Howard the librarian's unpleasant mugging in Saraton Township had helped him decide to look for a boat at Port Welton. How they had met was a story Charles enjoyed although he had never repeated it for fear Argo would have his head.

A year ago, Charles had been sent to the port city of Welton on an assignment to purchase a ship worthy of Argo's return to Saraton. Four boats were up for auction the day they met, bid on by forty men and one woman; two small boats only big enough for local transportation or fishing, an old navy ship without the cannons, and a ten-year-old ship with fully functional rigging and sails.

The two small boats and the rundown navy ship had gone quickly and for little money. But the ten-year old ship had three bidders, out of the thirty left. The tall bearded man stopped bidding after Charles had raised the bid to one thousand two hundred. The last bidder raised the total by ten, then Charles offered another fifty. They exchanged a couple counter bids before Charles removed his hat hoping to blend into the crowd. He approached the other bidder.

"Greetings. My name is Charles Cromwell."

"Nice to meet you. I am Howard Rochester."

Howard removed his hat to shake hands. Charles noticed the white streak running through Howard's black hair. Charles sneezed. "I need this boat for about two weeks. If I stop bidding, would you loan it or rent it to me for that time?" Charles asked.

"Do you have a trained crew to sail my ship?" Howard asked.

Charles paused momentarily. "No. I will have to find a crew." He hoped the arrangement was still possible.

Howard rubbed his chin for a few seconds.

"My crew sails the ship and you pay them four weeks' wages?"

"Okay," Charles replied. If the auction company discovers our private negotiation, they will sell our boat to the tall bearded man.

Howard whispered, "You know what we are doing is forbidden by the auctioneers?" He hesitated and glanced about. "What do you need my boat for?"

"Let me say that it would not be good for us to be caught." Charles was happy to find out Howard had a bit of larceny in his soul.

A sly smile wrinkled the corners of Howard's mouth. "We have a deal."

Charles sneezed. "Yes," he said, his voice immobilized by short gasps. He pinched his nose—the short gasps stopped. "But, I can only pay for two week's wages."

"Make it three, and we can call it a deal."

Charles nodded.

Howard raised Charles' last bid by ten.

* * *

Althea had time to prioritize her obligations and think through each possible outcome. Her duty was a late night escape to save Manshire and Kendrick.

Althea was surprised by her revelation that her greatest mentor for planning in the face of danger was Kendrick, who instantly used his mistakes to his advantage. He adapted to any dangerous situation moment-to-moment. She must be prepared for any surprises.

Althea began with the natural opening. I need something wider than the hole to tie a rope to.

The next afternoon, eating at the new table, she realized her resources included knowledge of the horses general location, weapons storage, that the soldiers slept every third night under the stars, and her two guards slept rather soundly for about three hours after the third candle was lit. Additionally, they were eager to please her in hopes that she remained happy and was less likely to risk escape—the condition she used to her advantage for the table. When she complained about eating with the plate on her knees, one of the guards brought a table.

Cromwell had been gone six days by Althea's count. She assumed routine and discipline were imposed conditions on any armed force—and had received six meals and eighteen candles since Cromwell's last visit. She carefully burned each candle to near the wicks end. In another three days she would have an extra full candle.

Althea's joy and fear had been confirmed the past two weeks. She did not have the runny nose or continual headaches shared by her chambermaid and natural mother. The ride from the castle to the cave had not merely tested her endurance but had drained her energy.

Althea rubbed her belly. *I must escape before Cromwell realizes he has kidnapped two.*

* * *

Cromwell arrived a day ahead of schedule. He approached Argo's tedious valet, "How is his mood today?"

"Okay, at best. His bath water was not hot enough."

"Tell him I am a day early and available to report our readiness. If he prefers tomorrow, I can return." *We really need a month...* his attention refocused as the heavy oak door opened just enough for the valet to squeeze through. Cromwell heard Argo's anger, "Why are the meats cold and the vegetables hot?"

For Cromwell, the sweat was building while the door remained closed. He looked around the room and scratched his head after he had counted nine white marble centaur statues.

He had counted the knots in the wood doors before the valet returned. "Go right in. He is excited to see you. And...you might have saved the cook's hand."

"Good day my king," Cromwell said entering the room. He stared at the floor.

"Charles, come sit with me." Argo raised his voice and spoke to no one in particular. "I hope you like cold meats and hot vegetables." He returned his attention to Cromwell, "How was your trip?"

"Good, I was able to see each camp and assess their readiness," Charles replied.

Argo's attention shifted to the butler, "Well, where is his food?"

"I will check sire," the butler replied.

"Make it quick if you wish to keep your hands," he hollered, then in the next instant, a calm voice directed at Charles, "Are we ready?"

"We are ready!" Charles said without hesitation—a talent he had mastered to avoid Argo's public and demeaning reprimands.

"Excellent answer. We should celebrate with wine."

Cromwell thought, if we must. Argo's low tolerance for wine was common knowledge among the staff.

Cromwell closed his lips on the goblet's edge as he drank, consuming about half a goblet to Argo's ten.

"You know why we are taking Saraton back?"

"Yes, my lord. It is the rightful property of your father."

"Yes, and, Manshire killed my brother when they invaded our homeland."

"I am sorry. This is the first time I have heard of this." Charles lifted his goblet to drink and was surprised by Argo's awkward clacking of Cromwell's goblet. "More wine for my friend."

Cromwell was well aware of the older brother's death and that suspicion surrounded the story. He did know that the older brother had either retreated or had been shot in the back during battle. Considering Argo's arrogance, Cromwell believed a soldier had been paid to end the prince's rise to kingship.

The second bottle was opened—the first bottle had slurred Argo's speech and jumbled his stories. At times, Cromwell had difficulty following them.

"And there is the step-queen Xage (zh-age). She took my money and I want it back," Argo said.

"How much did she get away with?" Cromwell asked.

"An abundant amount. Let me say it would be enough to make you king, of another country, of course." He took a long drink of wine. "We need to find and hide her for she can unravel our whole plan."

"Yes, my king. Is she still alive?" Cromwell had heard pieces of the story, but was unable to assemble the whole account.

Argo slammed his goblet on the table. It broke into several pieces. He wiped his hands down his shirtfront.

Typical Argo.

"Oh, and don't forget Camilla's involvement. Her selfish desires nearly bankrupted our little exiled kingdom." A servant handed him a fresh, full goblet, then cleared the broken pieces and running wine. "My money skills have kept us from ruin!"

Cromwell hoped he was about to finally hear the hushed Camilla story. "Who is Camilla?" he asked, hoping to keep Argo from drifting to another story.

"I am going to tell you a story that nearly dismantled the family... Except for you," he pointed at the servant with the ready goblet. "All servants leave the room." Argo took a long drink of wine and wiped his mouth with his shirtsleeve.

"Before I forget, make arrangements for the assassinations of Oscar, Quentin, Kendrick, and Althea. I want complete destruction of Manshire." Argo flipped his hand in the air like he was shooing a pesky fly. "Good wine."

Cromwell had been with Argo a long time and had grown accustomed to his daring proclamations. He had heard this commanded several times before—just today. Four assassinations sent his head spinning. It took all of his energy to remain expressionless.

Argo continued, "My mother died a few years after King Louis III invaded Saraton. I was twelve at the time. Father, in exile, married Xage the widowed Queen of Ruzler. She had much money, or so she said. I overheard father say he thought her fortune would save us. Then he found out she had married him for the same reason. Reality found father's stressed heart a few weeks later."

Cromwell knew part of Xage's legendary disappearance, a few sketchy stories about her trying to outwit Argo, and the rumors of the younger brother spying while hidden in Xage's armoire. Also, he had heard rumors that the King was driven by wishes and not good judgment. He leaned forward in his chair.

"As I said earlier. That was today? Right?"

"Yes, my king," Cromwell answered without being sure of what Argo was referring.

"My older brother died in the invasion, placing Camilla in line for the throne. She was witless, undisciplined, and careless with money—all the characteristics that brought fear to the step-queen." His arms whipped about as his temper flared, then settled by his goblet as his emotions chilled. "Xage bartered a marriage for Camilla in exchange for money from the new King of Ruzler. She was a conniving witch," Argo said. He took another long drink and stained the other sleeve. "Actually, danger lived near both women." His eyes closed.

While waiting, Cromwell thought about earlier in their relationship when Argo had seemed smart and prudent. Lately, he was just as smart, but in a scary, selfish, and intolerant way. Cromwell knew he was two too many goblets, from hearing the remainder of the story. He stood, looked at the servant, patiently waiting to replace Argo's goblet. "Is he asleep?"

The servant pointed at his ear and shook his head. He was deaf. A moment later he pointed to Argo.

Cromwell returned to his chair.

"More wine!" Argo said. "Camilla was in love with a painter and fought Xage. Charles, you need to drink more."

"Camilla?"

"Oh yes...as you might have guessed, the painter was penniless. Xage approached me with a plan to rid the royalty of Camilla. I would become king. All I had to do was to arrange Camilla's disappearance, and the step-queen would add some money to the royal treasury." Argo took a deep breath. His head fell forward onto the table. He was asleep now. The king's snoring sounded like an avalanche.

Typical Argo. He has something interesting to say and falls asleep. What happened to Camilla? Where did Xage get the money for the treasury? What happened to Xage the step-queen?

Cromwell returned to his room, lay on the bed, and attempted to sort all the story morsels.

Argo was such an imp—the last words that Cromwell remembered before sleeping.

The following morning, Cromwell hoped to finish breakfast quickly to avoid Argo. Another thing Argo was known for—being a royal grouch if he had spirits' morning nausea.

Cromwell did not eat fast enough. The dining room door swung open rapidly and would have crushed anything in its arch. "Where is my coffee?" Argo's voice echoed through the empty halls. As far as Cromwell could tell, the only servant on duty was the deaf goblet carrier.

King Argo was still staggering, nearly falling, partly because he trod on his cloak about every fourth step, his arms slowly swinging to the next chair, post, table edge, or wall that kept him from crashing.

"Coffee!" he yelled, then covered his ears. An instant later the lone servant appeared with piping hot coffee. A shaky sip momentarily calmed his belligerent bellowing as some of the brew dribbled out of the goblet. Argo wiped his chin. Cromwell wondered if the blue and orange colors that developed on his sleeves came from sleeping in the wild flowers.

"Oh, by the way, I sent my two guards to Manshire with the ransom note...about an hour ago," King Argo said.

Lieutenant Charles Cromwell was furious, but again controlled his expression. There is nothing worse than being stabbed by a grouchy king after breakfast. "I see, why two guards?"

"They both know I will imprison them if they fail, and each will safeguard the other does not read the letter," Agro replied. He angrily stabbed an apple with a fork and took a couple of bites. A minute later he said, "I have one last detail for you to execute."

* * *

Mid-morning, riding back to his cave, his mind swirling like a cyclone. Cromwell wanted, but had precious little time to ponder if he had talked to Argo for perhaps the last time?

By mid-afternoon Cromwell was exhausted from the questionable death of Argo's older brother, Bernard vanishing, the mysterious disappearance of Xage, and last night's surprise that would probably be another unpleasant ending—for Camilla.

His headache pounded with the rhythm of the hooves. He had to focus on the next twelve to sixteen days to reposition the militia that included fourteen secret Saraton beach landings for the squadrons on Cyphera. Adding to his pounding head was the most difficult of tasks—preparations for battle against Manshire.

Clarity's Arrival

Kendrick was in the rose garden when he heard two soldiers yelling outside the gate, "We carry a letter for Oscar Winston the Captain of the Long Bows, and Priest Prince Quentin Benedict."

He leaned the hoe against a rose bush, gathered his weapons belt and bow, and walked toward the soldiers. Ten Long Bow knights exited the castle gate and formed a circle around the soldiers.

"Dismount if you wish. It may take a while to find Oscar," Kendrick said.

"I am Oscar's son. You can give the letter to me, and I will deliver it to Oscar forthwith." He wanted to take the letter by force, but thought it better to wait for Oscar.

"Sir, our orders are to deliver this letter only to Winston or Benedict, then wait for a response," a soldier replied.

A few minutes later Oscar arrived on his horse. The knights parted as Oscar approached the soldiers. "I am Oscar Winston. Do you carry a letter for me?"

"First, where did you find the kidnapped twins? And what color was the flag?"

"The twins were found at a campfire in the south eastern most point of the Dragon's Back area." Oscar reached into his shirt pulled out a piece of material. "The flag was orange."

The Long Bows drew their swords as the soldier reached into his shirt, removed the letter, and held it close to his chest. "We have orders to wait for a response from you."

"And if I say no?" Oscar asked.

"Your Queen Althea might die."

Oscar and Kendrick exchange glances. Kendrick's reaction was similar to his father's as their eyes widened and mouths partially opened. Every muscle in Kendrick's body was tingling. All the surrounding noise of the day disappeared for he was focused on the two soldiers.

"Agreed," Oscar said.

The soldier nudged his horse forward and extended the letter to Oscar. He placed the letter inside his shirt, and extended his arm to help Kendrick jump on the back of Oscar's horse.

"Wait here. We must find Quentin. We will return with our response shortly." He pointed to a Long Bow. "Get them some food and drink."

Oscar tugged the reins. Within a few moments they had entered the castle gate. It was then Kendrick asked, "I assume you want to read the letter away from the soldiers and have the freedom to counter any possibilities, but I am surprised by the offer of food and drink."

"I am buying some time. It takes awhile to get the food, return it to the soldiers, and wait while they eat. They have been riding hard. Did you notice the dust on their forehead was streaked? Hopefully, our kind gesture will work to our advantage if we need it."

"Interesting tactic."

"I will go to the kitchen to instruct them on any food preparations we might need later. You find Quentin then meet me in the Queen's throne room."

A minute later, Kendrick slipped off the back of the horse and Oscar continued toward the kitchen. Before entering the cathedral, Kendrick hesitated to watch Father read the letter.

A few seconds passed. Oscar opened the envelope. He pushed his hat back with a single finger under the bill, then slowly played with his grey and black beard. He then rubbed his forehead before turning the letter over. He shook his fist at the sky. Kendrick could not hear, but knew his father—"flaming dragons".

Kendrick entered the cathedral's living quarters door and climbed the stairs to the second floor. Quentin's door opened before Kendrick could knock.

"Oh! Hello Kendrick. This is a surprise."

"Ah, good morning. We just received a letter concerning Althea. Father has asked that we meet him in the Assembly Hall." He pointed in the general direction of the castle.

"Yes, it is faster to go back the way you came in."

At the bottom of the stairs, away from peering eyes, Quentin grabbed the edges of his tunic and ran toward the castle. Kendrick followed on his heels. Still, they attracted considerable attention as they ran through the short hall until the large oak doors protecting the Assembly Hall opened. Kendrick closed the doors and placed the crossbar in the hooks.

"Althea has been kidnapped, and is being held in exchange for Saraton!" Oscar said, "Let me read the letter!" He took a deep breath:

Oscar, Quentin,

I am King Argo Paxton, son of King Albert V. I have your Queen Althea Benedict and plan to exchange her for the land formerly known as Saraton. Additionally, Manshire will provide to Saraton:

-Monies needed to return Saraton to financial stability.

-The release of all Saraton prisoners.

-A promise from you not to burn or destroy any crops or animals upon your departure.

-And, other requirements to be presented upon your arrival.

Your attendance at my castle is required within the next eight days. You may travel with my messengers or use the map on the back.

Any attempt to rescue Queen Althea will be met with harsh retaliation.

Be sure your chosen representatives have the authority to implement our demands. Kendrick Winston cannot be one of your representatives.

King Argo I

Oscar held the letter for Kendrick and Quentin to see the map.

"Kendrick, do you have any inclination for why they specifically excluded you?" Oscar asked.

"No sir!"

"We need to find out why. It could be of advantage to us," Oscar said. He turned toward Quentin. "We need to make you king, if only on a temporary basis. Are you prepared to take the risk associated with being king and representing Manshire?"

Quentin stared at the floor. He shook his head. "This is unbelievable, but I am willing." He lifted his head and squared his shoulders. "We should get the archbishop to swear me in—today. I gave my oath to father that I would do my duty if Queen Althea could not perform hers."

Oscar felt it was an unfair position to put a sixteen-year old priest-in-training into; but every precaution must be tended. He detected Quentin was proud to be asked, but scared—not an indecisive type of fear, but a fear of unknown expectations.

"We can talk more later. You should go and set-up the coronation."

Quentin rubbed the back of his neck and sat on the edge of the chair. He looked deep in thought.

"Quentin, is there anything you want to say?" Oscar asked.

"I have a dilemma. I heard information in the confessional, which I think might be important to our success. But that was as a priest. Now I am the king. Can I break my oath?"

"As much as I would like to know what you have learned, we should not tease fate or higher powers, though it might not hurt while setting up the coronation with the archbishop, to find-out your obligations and restrictions."

"What if I said you need to talk with an old woman wearing a scarf which has a violet spot on one end?" Quentin replied.

Kendrick stared at the wall behind Oscar.

"What are you thinking?" Oscar asked.

"I know this lady. I occasionally meet her in the rose garden. She was there this morning and left when the two soldiers arrived." Kendrick said.

"Where does she live?" Oscar asked.

"Uncertain. We pass in the garden. She helps me when the roses are sickly."

"We get so close and yet are far away." He turned to Quentin, "What do you know of her?" he whispered.

"I have met her only once."

"I will have the sergeant search for her," Oscar said.

Kendrick unlocked the door, Quentin stepped out, then Kendrick reset the plank. "Victor may also know this lady. He informed me he escorted an old woman out of the market and advised her to seek the comfort of the confessional."

"Hmmm." Oscar stared out the window.

* * *

For the past three nights, Althea had slowly and quietly ripped her slip into long pieces. She disassembled then reassembled one of the chair's rope joints and estimated material of the cot.

The slip sections were wrapped around her waist—hopefully disguising the missing slip, and her expanding stomach.

Althea prepared to lift her new eating table but it was too heavy and awkward. She had to know it would not fall through the listening hole. Removing four slip strips, she soaked them in the water bucket, then placed one under each table leg. The water provided enough lubrication to drag the table across the smooth floor. Placing the table by the opening, she determined the tabletop would not fall into it.

A short candle was placed in the ladle.

Two strips were tied together, then tied to the top hook of the ladle. Carefully lowering the candle she was able to see further into the hole. It reminded her of the dirt tubes the dogs followed as they dug to catch rodents. The hole angled slightly to the right, away from the direction of the large main room. Slowly she raised the candle and placed it back on the rock covered in wax drippings.

She filled the ladle, poured it on the four slip strips, and strained to pull the table back into the original location, returning everything to its original position.

Lying on the cot she thought about her next tasks. Do I go into the hole, feet first or head first? Should I soak my clothes in water? How do I hang the ladle to free up my hands?

* * *

"Father, I need to meet with a new friend. He was a former prince of Saraton," Kendrick said.

"What do you know of this 'friend'?" Oscar asked.

"He was abandoned in the forest by his brother, Argo." Oscar raised his eyebrows. "Bernard survived a few years on food smuggled out of the castle, raised a wolf from a puppy, lives in the forest area around the Dragon's Back and he is illusive. He is old enough to have memories of the former Saraton royalty. And, I am hoping he is holding a grudge," Kendrick replied.

"How do you propose to find him?"

"I thought I might take Victor so we can cover twice as much territory."

Oscar paced for about half a minute then took a deep breath. "I need to talk with you about Victor. He reminds me of Hunter the assassin at the Knight Games—same physique, a matching birthmark on his shoulder, and a similar speech rhythm. He flinches slightly when I enter the barracks," Oscar said.

Kendrick slowly wiped his hand down his face, took a deep breath, then slowly exhaled. I dare not take any chances with Althea's safe rescue. "Then we should be very careful with him."

"I suggest we see if my suspicions are valid by testing his friendship."

"You have a plan, I think." A wry smile came with Kendrick's realization that his father had been thinking about this for a while.

"My thoughts were to execute a scheme to uncover his loyalties after we had rescued Althea. But, we cannot take any chances with your search for the wolf man. Sit, we need to develop a scheme."

* * *

Cromwell dismounted at the path to the cave opening. The horseman appeared from behind the boulders and took the horse to the hidden corral.

Inside the large room, the busy activity reminded him of ants. Walking through the maze of trainees, he saw his oldest friend and confidant. When they made eye contact, Cromwell nodded his head to the side. They met in the far back of the main room.

"How was your tour of the training areas?" Curtis asked.

"Enlightening. Generally most of the squads are ready or near ready. Team two is the most advanced. Your group is probably next. Two teams are far behind. Regardless of our readiness the ransom letter has been delivered. We need to prepare the two main squads for clandestine operations. This training will start in a few days and continue until the seven squads have been delivered to Saraton soil." Cromwell tugged on the skin under his chin.

"Was the king tired of waiting?"

"Somewhat, but I am convinced the royal family is running out of funds. It takes a lot of money to feed, train, and arm nine hundred soldiers." He stared at the wall behind Curtis.

"Now, can you tell me what our mission is?"

Cromwell looked into Curtis's eyes. "In about a week."

"You appear troubled."

"Have you noticed that those close to the king…" Cromwell stopped mid-sentence. "Never mind, I can deal with it."

"Maybe some grog will help you sleep. A good rest will refresh your body. It's camp out night—stars and grog, a wonderful combination."

"That sounds good. How is our hostage?"

"She is fine. No trouble," Curtis replied.

"She is more like Argo than she shows. You can be assured she is working on an escape plan." He rubbed his tired eyes. "Where is that grog?"

"I will return in a few minutes."

"No rush. I am going to visit Althea."

"Has the plan changed?"

"Slightly. We need her alive."

* * *

Oscar watched the sun slink above the horizon. His foul mood had grown worse with each sleepless night as he rehashed what he did not know. Then the ransom letter filled him with more questions about Althea's location and health. Could he find her before she was assassinated?

Sitting wrapped in his blanket, heels of his crossed legs on the window ledge, and his head nodding off to sleep, he would accept sleep for ten to fifteen minutes.

His dream of someone yelling at him ended abruptly when the sergeant burst through the barracks door. Oscar bolted from the chair, snatching his sword and knife; he was facing the door prepared to thrust his sword at the intruder. The door to his private sleeping quarters flew open as he heard, "It is me, my Captain. I found her. I found her."

Oscar lowered his weapons. "Her, who?"

"The lady with the purple spotted scarf."

"Where is she?"

"I left two Long Bows to watch her. They are helping her tend the rose garden."

"Take me to her."

A moment of joy wisped through him like the breeze's last draught—it was a new beginning...finally!

Oscar, the sergeant, and a handful of Long Bows ran to the garden. Oscar held up his hand as they drew near. "Let me talk with her alone. Wait here."

He noticed the roses and thought of the hours Abbey had spent cultivating her Amherst Spring roses. A tear wet his cheek. He took a deep breath.

"Gentlemen, I can take over for you," Oscar said. The two young knights nodded, gathered their bows, and were gone in an instant.

"What are we doing, and how can I help?"

"Well, I just finished aerating the root soil. There are a few dead stems to cut out. Feel like a few scratches?" The old lady said.

"What do I need to do?" He asked, but already knew.

"Use your knife and cut the leafless brown stems off as far down as your pain can endure."

Oscar removed his knife and clipped the first dead stem, then cut two more.

"You have done this before."

"Yes ma'am. My son transplanted these from our farm. They were my wife's favorite."

"Then you would be Oscar, Captain of the Guard."

"Correct." He cut another four stems and sheathed his knife. "What else needs tended to?"

"That is all for now. I promised your son I would take care of them. He hopes they do not bloom until the queen can see them. I have been trying to slow their growth without killing them."

"You know who I am, but I do not know your name."

"It is Xage."

"Well Xage, we have been looking for you in hopes that you might have information that we need to rescue the queen."

"I saw her ride out the gate. Did you know?" She teetered a few moments.

Oscar touched Xage's arm to steady her.

"Thank you," she said with a smile. "If you can avoid it, do not grow old—it is a tough way to live."

"Can I escort you somewhere?"

"I would like to go home."

Oscar extended his elbow. "Lead the way Xage."

Her single nod gave Oscar a confidence that quickly evaporated with the first few shaky steps.

He asked, "Do you mind if we talk about your sighting of the queen, and what you might know of her abductors?"

"Why? No one else would listen."

"They are young and do not have our patience." Oscar slowed his pace.

"Ask away. I will tell you what I know."

"Do you know King Argo Paxton?"

"He calls himself king. Hmmm. That is how he is, you know." She looked at Oscar's face. "I think he planned the deaths of his older brothers and sister to become, did you say, the king...? It happened so silently."

Oscar wanted to ask about the causes of their deaths, but presently he was concerned with the key elements should she fall asleep before he found out."

"What are Argo's strengths?"

"He is patient to a point, then he becomes a raving idiot— purely irrational. He could stab you then turn to kiss a baby. His emotional direction changes faster than a hummingbird."

"Yes, go on," Oscar whispered. He was growing impatient and had to remind himself of the importance of this interrogation—it had been nearly a week without a clue, another hour would not matter.

"He is a devious planner. There is always something behind what he reveals. If it is something he wants—he will have it before you know what happened. You might not ever figure out how he did it." She paused by a low wall. "Can we sit for awhile? This body needs lots of rest."

"Yes. I thought you would never ask."

Xage leaned forward placing her hands on her knees. She took a deep wheezing breath. Oscar worried she might die right there.

"Are you alright?" Oscar asked. He put his arm around her.

"You remind me of my first husband the King of Ruzler. Leonard was a good man. Not like Argo's Father Albert—he was a selfish man living a life of luxury at the kingdom's expense. Argo has those same traits, but Argo can be bribed—the little man is greedy."

"How do you know these things?"

"I was married to King Albert, the fifth, for a short time. Then after his death the royal family began to disappear. The oldest boy died in battle against you, us, Manshire. That actually happened before Albert died, leaving Camille and Bernard in line for the throne. Argo arranged for each to disappear. Scared, I fled to Manshire."

"I know of Bernard."

"Oh, he is still alive? He would fall asleep in my closet while gathering information for Argo. We knew when he was in the closet—Bernard snored when he was a young boy." She turned her head to look into Oscar's eyes. "I am so tired today, may I rest on your shoulder?

"Certainly, but I can arrange for a wagon to take you home," he whispered.

But, she was already asleep on his shoulder.

The Gambit

At sunrise, Oscar, the sergeant, six Long Bows, and Quentin the king pro tem left the castle gate and headed to a beach south of Port Welton to catch a boat to Cyphera. Oscar had decided to leave the government ministers in Manshire for their safety. He took additional Long Bows to protect Quentin.

The bright orange, purple, and yellow clouds warned of a storm. The brisk spring air felt good against his face as the horses trotted along the road.

Although the end of Althea's kidnapping affair was far off, Oscar felt a sense of relief, and happy they had finally found a beginning. He checked on Quentin. "Are you okay?"

"It is good to have a feeling of hope that we will bring Althea home soon," Quentin said. His voice was shaky.

"Yes, my king," Oscar said. At that instant, his sense of relief evaporated. Yes, my king resounded in his head. He was obligated to protect the king from every form of harm.

Quentin wore Oscar's hooded coat. The first raindrops soaked through Oscar's layered shirts. The rain made it difficult to be sure, however he saw beads of sweat gathering on Quentin's forehead. Oscar assumed Quentin was afraid of the unknown or that anyone who had the courage to plan a queen's abduction might decide to abduct him. Oscar decided he would lift Quentin's confidence with knowledge.

"Quentin, as the king, you need to be the main spokesman at the proceedings. While we ride, we should discuss your tactics and boundaries."

'That would be much appreciated. I do not want to endanger Althea or Manshire on a mistake." His chin was shaking.

Oscar used a calm even voice to relax Quentin. "When we arrive, I expect Argo to be bold and confident; thinking he is in control. This behavior could start early. Perhaps it is as simple as they do not hold the door for you. But, regardless we need to be prepared to challenge him from the start." Oscar had moved his horse slightly ahead of Quentin to watch his reactions. "As the new king you can demand your royal expectations be met. Argo's people will expect that because he is that way. This behavior will also let him know you are someone who must be treated with respect." He was pleased with the raised eyebrows of Quentin's slightly tilted head.

"What if he becomes angry?"

"Be tranquil. Do not get upset. You need to keep him off balance and as uncomfortable as possible. Be prepared to say things that you have no intention of doing for the sake of control—I know you are a priest, but you can ask for forgiveness later."

Quentin's head steadily nodded, though it looked like a raccoon was loose in the hood.

"What else? This is very helpful."

Oscar glanced at the sergeant and pointed at a split in the road using three fingers. The sergeant nodded, tugged left on the reins, and separated from the group.

He turned to resume the conversation as Quentin abruptly asked, "Why is he leaving us?"

"A security check." Oscar paused in case Quentin needed further explanation. "You need to exploit his weaknesses: greed, selfishness, ego, and emotional instability. He will say or do anything to achieve his goals. Here is what we know of Argo—the kidnapping of the twins was a ruse so he could abduct the queen." He let that float in Quentin's mind for a minute. "We must be careful with this Argo. His plans have been well executed and quite deceptive. I suspect his spies will be watching us at all times." Oscar did not want to discuss how Argo had had Bernard hide in Xage's closet.

"We need a few signals to communicate without talking." Oscar placed his index finger and thumb on his chin. "For example, 'this' means we want or need to think about it. If I pull on my ear lobe, it means the same thing."

When his eyebrows lifted, Quentin's forehead wrinkled. "Why the duplicate signals?

"It is intended to keep Argo from discovering we are signaling."

The rain had stopped. Quentin pushed the hood off his head. "Whew, this coat is hot." He glanced toward Oscar. "Can you tell me how the first day will unfold?"

"Argo will begin with some additional demands—he implied that in his letter. He hopes to frustrate us. Be prepared for him to leave the room. If he does, we do too."

"Why? That will lead to Althea's..." Quentin's face turned white.

"He can not hurt her. He needs her alive to keep us at the negotiating table—which also means we will need to keep from reaching a conclusion to ensure she remains alive. Once the deal is done, she is dead! Unless we can tempt him with a prize."

"Remember we are gathering information that leads to Althea," Oscar said. Quentin rubbed his temples with the middle finger and thumb of his left hand. "Not to worry, we have four days to perfect your performance."

Quentin's partial, uncertain smile came and went.

* * *

Kendrick rode through the castle gate an hour after Oscar. He wore his olive green felt hat with a brown pheasant feather, light grey shirt, dark grey pants, and a deerskin-hooded coat. The horse, a light buckskin color with a dark chestnut mane, tail, and knee high socks.

Following the same road as his father, at the split Kendrick directed the horse to the left.

He was invigorated. The chilly rain had started again but it could not quench the fire in his soul. He was happy to be productively pursuing Althea's return.

Three miles after the road separation he found the sergeant waiting. They saluted. The sergeant wore an olive green felt hat with a brown pheasant feather, light brown shirt, dark grey pants, and a deerskin-hooded coat. The horse's dark chestnut mane was a striking contrast to its light buckskin color and reddish brown tail. Its ankle high socks were covered in mud.

Kendrick rode into the forest about a quarter mile, dismounted, and ran to the top of a small hill. A few minutes passed before Kendrick spotted the rider. The rain had its advantages and problems—it destroyed the hoof prints making the follower ride closer than normal, but it left no margin for error or indecision for anyone being followed.

Moments later he signaled the sergeant who tapped his horse's flank and rode away.

Kendrick lowered his head and pressed his lips. He thought about their afternoon hunting trips, the evening dinners at the castle, and the night they laughed so hard Victor fell off the chair. He felt like he had lost a brother.

After a few moments he lifted his head feeling safer knowing Victor would be captured in a few miles by the sergeant and one of the Long Bows riding with father.

Kendrick walked his horse back to the road, glanced in the direction of the sergeant's trap, shook his head, and then rode off toward the split—following the same road Oscar had traveled an hour before.

After a long ride, he arrived at Dragon's Back, the same location where Oscar and Kendrick had divided the rescue group into two teams chasing the twins' kidnappers.

He dismounted, retrieved the clay pot hanging on the saddle, and dug a hole. He placed a couple pieces of charcoal, a deer hide provided by Oscar, and a large piece of tanned leather inside the vessel. Gently he positioned it in the hole, set the cap, and laid a piece of deer hide over the pot. He covered everything with dirt and smoothed out the surrounding soil. Three paces due north and past the edge of the trail, a short length of green cloth stuck out from beneath a large stone.

Kendrick was satisfied with his task. He took a deep breath, briefly studied the forest, and then began his search for Bernard.

* * *

The sergeant kept his hood on, but the rain had stopped. He dismounted, removed his long bow, shouldered the quiver, and waited against a tree to improve his footing. The half grey sky helped hide him in the darkened forest.

Ten minutes passed. Victor rode around the curve of the slightly inclined road, leaning over the horse's neck checking the wet ground for tracks. It was too late when he noticed the sergeant with his bow drawn. He was preparing to yank the reins in the other direction when a Long Bow slid on the wet clay into the middle of the road behind him.

"Halt!" the sergeant yelled.

Victor continued to alternate glances in both directions.

"Are you considering escape against two trained Long Bows?"

Victor raised his hands to chest high.

"Drop the reins and dismount," the sergeant said, sliding toward Victor. "Slowly."

"I will lose my balance trying to dismount with my hands held high."

The sergeant lost his balance momentarily. He was afraid that Victor's youthful fearlessness and their unstable footing would motivate Victor to attempt an escape.

A wry smile accompanied Victor's rapid glances at both men before he kicked the horse's hips.

Before gaining control, the sergeant released his arrow that entered below Victor's shoulder. He watched the Long Bow's arrow disappear into the forest.

The sergeant's muddy feet slipped with nearly every step; several times he had to extend his arms for balance. Attempting to fly another arrow before Victor was out of range, he lost traction landing face first into the mud. He heard the Long Bow's horse gallop by.

He had wiped the mud from his eyes and nose. Covered in mud, he made his way to the side of the road to a log and wiped the slick clay from his clothes with small branches.

Five minutes later, the Long Bow returned with a bleeding arm.

"What happened?" the sergeant asked.

"He stopped and turned toward me. At the last moment, he looked to the sky, and then I think he re-aimed at my arm. Does that make any sense to you?" the Long Bow replied.

"No, but we must bandage that arm before we give chase," the sergeant said. Victor had very good skills. He was obviously trained.

* * *

Following the same trail he had taken to the ambush. Kendrick was making good progress. Through the brush and boulders he saw the two stone monuments covering the dead Long Bows, and enemy archers. As he rode by, he could not take his watery eyes off the graves. His stomach burned.

He continued on for an hour and a half. At dusk he camped and ate the white-eared possum he had shot earlier.

Kendrick was ready at dawn. He stirred the coals with dirt then continued east for three hours. The rock formation known as Dragon's Back slipped into the earth. There was a peaceful view of the ocean on the horizon, which he enjoyed for a few minutes.

He walked around the end of Dragon's Back. A two-foot wide dirt patch along the edge was protected from the rain by a rock overhang.

Wolf tracks.

His heartbeat increased as he followed the tracks. Occasionally, he saw Bernard's small footprints. The tracks led into a boulder field. Five minutes later he walked upon a small grassy meadow with a clear water pond. Right before him was a cave opening with manmade doors. Things were starting to improve.

When Kendrick turned toward the cave, a half growl followed instantly by a soft bark. His heart raced.

Exeter?

Slowly Kendrick turned.

"Hello," Bernard said. "Exeter says hello too."

"Bernard I am happy it is you."

"Come Kendrick, to my humble cave." He pointed at a path worn through the grass.

Bernard held out his arms. "Within a month this meadow will be spring green—a wonderful time of year. What brings you here?"

"I am hoping you do not think me imposing on our fresh friendship, but can you provide me with information about Argo? He has kidnapped our queen and is holding her for a large land swap—the former country of Saraton."

"Wow, that is a bold and large ransom," Bernard replied. "Do you plan to pay?"

"I am uncertain. The king and captain of the guard are traveling to a beach near Port Welton to board a boat for Cyphera. They represent Manshire." Kendrick felt uncomfortable giving Bernard his prepared answer. He turned away momentarily to see hundreds of trout in the pond. "You must eat a lot of fish."

With the enthusiasm of a puppy, Bernard said, "Surprisingly, the pond does not freeze in the winter. You are only my third visitor—ever. Are you hungry? We can talk while eating." Bernard extended his hand toward the cave entrance.

"Sure. That would be nice."

"You can sit here." Bernard gestured at a large, flat rock next to an unusual table. "I made the table last winter. Carpentry is not one of my best skills." Bernard cut meat off what looked like a wild turkey leg. "Try this. I cooked it this morning."

The cave opening was partially covered with panels of log poles lashed together with bark strips—they looked like rafts standing on end. Kendrick felt his hat rub the ceiling occasionally. The solid rock cave was made from a light grey molten matter with black pepper like chips. Along a flat section of the floor was a bookshelf made of woven willow branches. It held six books, a large pinecone, some unusual rocks, a wolf carving, and a shiny metal helmet. The bed was a collection of grass and was contained by four logs forming a square—about three feet from the fire ring. On the other side of the fire was a basket for food. The room was ample, compact, practical, and efficient—a reflection of its resident.

"How did you learn to start a fire, construct the walls, and gather food when the supplies quit coming?" Kendrick asked.

Bernard walked to the bookshelf, removed a hand written copy of Survival Skills for Manshire Long Bows by Oscar Winston. Kendrick skimmed a few pages. It was fifty-seven pages of how to start a fire, build a shelter, a snow cave, how to select safe natural foods, and so on. Kendrick stared at Bernard, turned some pages then returned his gaze to Bernard.

"Where did this come from?" Kendrick's fingers rubbed his cheek.

"I am uncertain. It came with what turned out to be the last supply of food." Bernard looked at the ground and scratched his head. "I am taking time away from your questions, sorry. I am so excited to have company."

"I understand." Kendrick thought of the time he had managed the farm alone. "What can you tell me about Argo that may help us rescue our queen?"

"Be very careful where Argo is concerned—he is a master of deception. What you see is not what he has planned. Do you know of Camilla and the step-queen, Xage?" Bernard paused, taking a bite of meat. While wiping his hands he continued. "Xage was afraid Camilla would become queen for she was legally the next in line after the oldest son's death. Camilla was in love with a local painter, and gave money to anyone that had the courage to ask and the painter had courage. Xage was just the opposite, a money hoarder. She had buried money removed from her previous royal position." He handed a goblet of water to Kendrick then poured water into his cupped hand and slurped.

"To feed her fear Xage struck a deal with Argo—she would give money to the exiled kingdom if he would prevent Camilla's rise to queen. A few weeks later he sold her to the gypsies."

"Xage, true to her word, gave Argo a healthy sum of money in a wooden box covered with dirt. So much gold that Argo made me responsible to find out if she had other money, or Argo would 'feed me to the wolves.' At the time, Argo was a foot and a half taller, plus much stronger. He forced me into the closet to spy on conversations between Xage and her chambermaid. I followed her one night. She dug up a box and removed a bag of gold coins. Covered the box again. Strangely, she pointed in mid-air three times. It was not until Argo threatened me that I figured out she was counting the other boxes."

He pointed at the food basket, "More?"

"Yes, please. It is very tasty. What happened next?"

"Foolishly, I tried to negotiate with Argo. I would tell him where the boxes were if he left me alone. Argo left me alone—in the wilderness at fifteen."

"Did you ever find out who sent the food?"

"I believe it was Xage's chamber maid. There were letters and notes that came with the food over the three years. One stated Xage had secretly left the country to a safe location. I had thought Xage brought the food, but after that note the food kept coming." He looked down at his boots. He took a deep breath. A few seconds passed before he raised his head.

"That is a powerful story," Kendrick said. "I am impressed with your survival skills."

"It was your father's book that saved my life."

"How did you know Oscar was my father?"

"I have my ways."

* * *

Oscar, Quentin, and the knights arrived early afternoon after three long days of riding—just to wait on the southernmost beach of what may once again become Saraton.

The white sands began at the grassy edge of the forest with a four-foot drop to the beach. At low tide, it was a two-minute walk to the ocean's fringe, which gradually shortened throughout the day. Fifty yards to the west a creek ran full into the ocean washing away sand to form a seventeen-foot basin.

Oscar spent the day with Quentin rehearsing various replies to anticipated behaviors from Argo. He was thankful for the hours spent with Xage, and felt they had a chance of saving Althea.

Dusk would start soon. Wood for the campfire had been gathered and two Long Bows prepared to skin a couple of rabbits. Oscar wanted to be sure Quentin did not have any distractions resulting from hunger.

"Do you see a ship on the horizon?" Oscar asked, while pointing at the ship.

"Yes sir," replied a Long Bow. "I believe it is traveling this direction."

"I hope this is our ship."

For half an hour, they watched the ship come closer then anchor. Several rowboats were lowered to the water followed by men descending on nets. Three boats were rowed toward the basin. A few minutes later four more boats, appearing from the ship's starboard, followed them.

Oscar sent Quentin and the Long Bows into the forest to protect the king. Five minutes later, two men jumped from the lead boat and pulled it to shore. Three men approached Oscar. Each had shortened pants, sleeveless shirts, and bandanas tied around their necks. The shortest man rubbed his thin beard. The tallest sailor scratched his baldhead. The third man removed a hat revealing his red hair.

"We are sent by Captain Howard Rochester of the ship Rightful Belle to collect Oscar Winston, Quentin Benedict, and three ministers," said the short man.

Where have I heard this captain's name before? Oscar thought

"Who might you be?" asked Red-hair.

"I am who you seek, Oscar Winston."

"We sail tonight to Cyphera," said Red-hair

Oscar raised his hand to signal the knights. They appeared from the forest and moved through the grass with bows drawn."

"Sir, we have no weapons, and no harm will come to you. I swear. Let me show you a letter from Argo," Red-hair said.

Oscar read the letter, then stretched his arm to the side and slowly let it drop—the Long Bows lowered their weapons. "Who are the men in the boats?"

"They are business with another customer."

It was an answer that Oscar did not like, but he did not pursue clarification, as this was the ship they had waited for.

Quentin arrived at the beach a few moments after the Long Bows. "How long to our destination?" he asked. His back was straight, head was held high, and his shoulders were back. A tone of arrogance filtered through the air.

"After we weigh anchor, about six hours," replied Red-hair.

"And what of our accommodations on your boat?"

"Sir, it is a ship." Red-hair pointed. "Those are boats."

"And when do we board your ship?" Quentin's tone was creeping toward indignant.

"A boat waits on the beach for your grace."

"And our accommodations?"

"You can stay in my cabin," Red-hair said. The other two men smiled.

"Very good. Oscar you are with me. Two knights in front and back. Lead the way to your row boat," Quentin commanded.

As the sailors walked to the boat, Oscar covered his mouth to hide a smile. He winked at Quentin.

"Who are those...?" Quentin asked, before Oscar interrupted.

Oscar pulled on his earlobe. Quentin winked, he would ask his questions later.

Four sailors with oars waited at the boat. Oscar boarded so he could help Quentin. The oarsmen boarded, followed by two leaders as the bald man pushed the boat from shore.

Oscar and Quentin, at the back of the boat, faced the oarsmen, while the three leaders faced forward. "Are you going back to take charge of loading the militia?" a sailor asked Oscar.

"Row and stop talking," Red-hair said.

Half way to the ship, Quentin looked ashen. His short hums as he squeezed his stomach caught Oscar's attention. "Are you okay, my king?"

"I will be fine."

A few seconds passed and Quentin stuck his head over the side of the boat.

"Sea sick?" Red-hair laughed. The other sailors joined in the laughter.

Oscar smiled. Quentin's transformation into the new king was successful. He had managed to irritate them and quickly develop into the perfect young king to battle Argo.

* * *

Bernard described three possible locations good for hiding a few soldiers and a kidnapped queen. The first possible location was Brackish Cave, a small place and a two-day hike in rugged country. The next suggestion was Ocean Hollow where the entrance was hard to secure; he assumed Argo would not hide Althea in a location with multiple escape routes.

Kendrick decided to check Whistling Forest—with its huge underground cave labyrinth and a hidden entrance. Bernard had thought about living there, but with each rain a musty sulfur odor filled the chambers and the wind made an awful noise.

Bernard's hand drawn map had delivered Kendrick to the outlook point above the cave's entrance. Kendrick folded the leather carefully to minimize any smearing of the charcoal on the leather.

A well-travelled path intersected a larger trail near several large boulders. A man was hiding within the four large rocks like he was guarding the entrance to a cathedral. Why would someone want or need to be there? Ten minutes lapsed before anyone used the path. From the boulders the hidden man waived to the archer then ran off. Odd behavior. A minute went by. The cathedral guard returned with a horse. The archer nodded and rode away.

An hour later he heard uproar through the trees—like men cheering—reminding Kendrick of the Knight Games patrons. He looked to the sky—two more hours before dusk. Dark clouds were gathering in the west. He slowly digressed from the lookout point.

Kendrick removed his hat. His graceful movements permitted a quiet passage through the thick undergrowth toward the ruckus. He crawled on his belly and then carefully peered over the rock hedge. Eighty-plus men were training in hand-to-hand combat, swordplay, and archery. Why? If Althea was here, why would so many men guard against her escape?

Startled by a bugle, Kendrick cringed. He peeked over the hedge and saw the group walking toward the cave's entrance.

He worked his way back to the lookout. The noise escaping through the entrance was similar to that of a weekend pub. An awful whistling sound covered the cave clatter with each wind gust.

The moon would soon be rising out of the long sunset shadows.

A familiar rider stopped at the boulders. As though he saw a ghost, an unnerving twinge travelled through Kendrick's muscles.

* * *

The sun had cleared the horizon when the ship bumped the dock at the closest port near Venela. After the crew lashed the ship's ropes around the cleats, the gangplank was extended to the dock.

The activity woke Oscar who had slept on deck against the anchor winch. Laid out on the deck about five feet away, Quentin slept through the commotion.

Red-hair asked Oscar, "Are you going to wake him? Or can I do it?"

"No. I'll wake him. Otherwise, he will be unbearable all day."

"I understand. Wake him soon, we do not have much cargo to load and stow."

Oscar stood and stretched. A large group of men suddenly appeared from a barn across the field. He knelt down and shook

Quentin's shoulder. "Wake up. I could use your help," he whispered.

Quentin rubbed his eyes. "Sure, what do I need to do?"

"Your new king act. Walk off the ship, down the dock, and see if you can find out what those men are doing." Oscar pointed his finger at his shoulder, but Quentin knew he was hiding the gesture. He leaned out to look around Oscar.

"Oh my," Quentin whispered. "A boat load of men. Like last night." He stood and stretched. "Okay, wish me luck."

Quentin had crossed the gangplank, and was a few feet down the dock when Red-hair, leaning over the side, shouted at him, "Stop there. You must be escorted."

"Okay, I will be over there waiting for you to escort me." He pointed toward the beginning of the dock—ten feet from the gathering men.

"I will get him," Oscar said. He prepared to step onto the gangplank when a familiar voice shouted, "Halt. I am captain Howard Rochester. I will have you shot if you do not stop."

Oscar turned to see two archers and the captain—the unmistakable white streak in his hair. "You were the librarian."

"Yes. Now I am the captain." He moved to within whispering distance of Oscar. "This little performance was staged for your benefit." He stepped back, looked at Red-hair, and said, "Get them off my ship. Now." He smiled at Oscar then departed for the bridge.

* * *

"What did you find out?" Oscar asked.

"They are going to Saraton, and will be paid in gold for their service. I think that is all they know," Quentin replied.

A black carriage pulled by two white horses, arrived twenty minutes after the ship had left the dock. "Gentlemen, Argo sends his carriage for you." The driver pointed at the door.

"It is hard to be the new king when your expectations are surpassed by Argo sending his carriage." Quentin boarded the carriage. Oscar followed, closed the door, and sat down.

A half hour ride in the carriage ended in front of an old stone construction winery marked by a tile plaque as the Kingdom of Saraton. The old thatch roof had been replaced with wooden shake shingles. A rose bush on each side of the entrance reminded Oscar of the rose garden in Manshire. The grounds were well maintained.

The driver placed a step below the open carriage door. Quentin continued his harassing antics, "About time. Thank you anyway." The driver offered his hand to assist him, which was met with a scolding tone, "I am not a child."

Two wide steps provided access to the entrance. Two guards dressed in colorful yellow, red, and blue uniforms, holding long metal tipped wooden spears, opened the palace doors.

The entry hallway was quite plain with a few soot-darkened tapestries hanging behind three stone centaur statues. At the end of the hallway was a double oak arched door. From the doorway came the confident tenor of a young man standing with his hands on his hips.

"This way gentlemen."

Oscar bowed and extended his arm to show servitude toward Quentin—wondering if he had created a dragon. At the door, Quentin nodded at a young man of about his same age.

Two swords crossed in front of Oscar before he entered the four-foot hallway. "Your weapons," one of the guards commanded.

"He keeps his weapons or we leave," Quentin replied.

Both guards looked to the young man, who waved his arm in disgust. "Okay."

"Close the doors."

After latching the door, a guard moved to each end of the room.

Oscar thought it odd for Argo, the paranoid king, to have a meeting room with two large oval mirrors on each wall. But Argo was also the master planner, and undoubtedly used them to artfully manipulate others.

Argo slapped the table and his tone changed dramatically. "I am Argo. I am not a patient king and insist you meet my requirements forth with. I have added a few demands since delivering the letter; free trade between Saraton and Manshire, free portage at the Manshire port, twenty percent of Manshire's crops for the next four years. And, oh yes, return the king's hunting lodge."

"Free trade and portage is reasonable. The hunting lodge is of no use to us. But, twenty percent of our crops is outrageous!" Quentin said.

"Can we settle at fifteen percent then?" Argo asked. He had not sat yet. He tried to hide a sly smile by turning away, but Oscar saw his face in the reflection.

Before Oscar could give the "no" sign, Quentin replied, "we can settle at no percent.

Argo stood across the table from Quentin, placed both hands on the edge, and stared at him. The king pro tem sat back in the chair, leaned on one elbow, and returned a relaxed stare. It was subtle, but Argo flinched—as if he had expected something different from Quentin.

"I have spent many hours thinking about this and my offer is more than fair."

"You spent many hours and your assessment is exactly twenty percent, not eighteen percent, or nineteen point three percent?" Quentin responded.

Argo leaned forward. "It is twenty percent or your queen Althea dies."

Quentin slowly stood, placed his hands on the table, and leaned to about a foot from Argo. "Go ahead. I am king now and I say we are prepared to resolve this on the battlefield."

Argo took a deep breath, looked at Oscar, and asked, "Do you have anything to add?"

Oscar was impressed with Argo's style. "No. He is my king."

"Well then, we are in agreement—the queen is no longer of any use and can be eliminated."

He glanced at the guard by the door. "Notify Cromwell that she can be dispatched." Still leaning on the table Argo looked into Quentin's eyes. "My demands will be met or you will never leave this room alive."

Quentin's calm facade did not waiver meeting Argo eye to eye.

Oscar's fatherly pride triggered a smile that lasted only moments as he witnessed Argo's anger intensify. He checked the guards; the sentry at the door pulled his knife. Oscar stood, threw his knife, and pinned the guard's fluffy yellow sleeve to the wall.

In the mirror he saw the second guard moving rapidly preparing to spear him, but Oscar lifted the chair to block the spearhead. He reached around the chair grabbing the spear shaft and yanked it free. He snapped the shaft over his knee and laid the spearhead on the table.

The guard removed his knife and lunged. With his forearm, Oscar pushed the knife hand toward Argo, grabbed the guard's wrist, placed his other hand on the guard's shoulder, and slammed his head into the table edge.

Oscar gathered the spearhead and placed it against Argo's throat.

For a brief period the room was silent before others started banging on the doors, shouting, "Are you all right King Argo?"

Argo's voice was silent, but from the corner of his eye he stared at Oscar.

Oscar moved the spearhead off Argo's throat and lifted one eyebrow while tilting his head. If I could assure my king's safe passage, and return of the queen, I would end this right now.

"Yes. Yes, fine." Argo replied.

Oscar set the spearhead on the table. Argo alternated glances at Quentin, Oscar, and the spearhead.

"Do not attempt. I can end this for you with an arrow," Oscar said. He pointed to his quiver that was now resting on the table. Oscar stared at Argo. He sat. "We need a good faith gesture or we will leave!"

"Guards, leave the room."

Quentin wiped his palms on his pants as they sat.

"Another thing. Get rid of the people behind the mirrors," Oscar said.

Argo lifted his hand and flipped his wrist twice. Sounds similar to large scurrying rats filtered through the walls.

"We are okay with your offer including the crops at only ten percent, but only if Althea is escorted to Manshire unharmed," Quentin said.

Oscar was surprised as Quentin was in negotiating territory they had not discussed. He worried they might lose complete control of the meeting and opportunity to extend the deadlines for Kendrick to rescue Althea. He interrupted Quentin to play the 'insurance' gambit.

"My king, if I may," Oscar said. Quentin nodded his head. "We are willing to exchange the location of a healing pond for Althea's safe return. The pond would let you enjoy the pleasures of being King for many extra years."

Argo was silent. He stood and paced.

When he stopped pacing, Oscar could sense Argo was enchanted—he stared at the ceiling with his palm resting on his chin while his first finger tapped his cheek.

"How do I validate that the pond truly has healing powers?" Argo asked.

Oscar wanted to say 'we could injure you' but decided against it. "I will stay here until your men verify the location of the pool. When they return in eight days, you send a messenger to escort my queen to Manshire castle. Your escort returns with my sergeant. Then, the sergeant and I leave you to rule Saraton."

"I will need some time to think about your offer. We will arrange for some food and accommodations. We can finish tomorrow." Argo's voice had a boyish tone, and his arms swung like exaggerated pendulums as he left the room. Oscar saw the smile in the mirror.

Quentin faced Oscar, "Now what?"

Oscar held a single finger against his lips. "We wait."

Unspoken Truths

The guard that Oscar had slammed into the table's edge awakened him and Quentin. Oscar's first thought was the guard planned to harm them, but the guard held up empty hands. "Argo is ready to continue, please follow me."

When the guard turned, Oscar slipped a piece of leather into the pocket of his jacket.

There was silence as they walked to the meeting room.

Inside, Argo paced by the window.

Oscar hoped the gloomy weather was not an indication of Argo's mood. After the door closed, he stopped pacing and faced Quentin.

"No need to sit, I accept your offer. But, if this turns into a ruse, I will kill Oscar myself." He stared out the window a few seconds. "Quentin we will escort you to the dock, but cannot provide protection."

"No problem, I have men waiting for me at the beach."

"I have ordered my carriage for you. You should go. The next boat is leaving soon."

Oscar walked Quentin to the carriage. Once outside Oscar whispered, "After you are on the ship, check the coat pocket." As the carriage jerked forward, Quentin waived, and held Oscar's coat in his other hand.

When the carriage was out of sight, Argo and two guards met Oscar on the steps.

"Seize him!" Shouted Argo. "And resume the troop transport to Saraton."

* * *

Traveling back to the Whistling Forest lookout Kendrick had time to determine if there was evidence to support Althea being held at Whistling Forest. Why does Saraton need so many men to guard Althea? Father was correct—Victor was one of them. The cave complex was enormous and could be an ideal location to hold a queen.

A rider approached the boulders. The stableman saluted the rider, then led the horse toward the outdoor stable under the rock overhang that Kendrick had found yesterday.

The large rider briskly walked toward the cave entrance. Two men on the path saluted the rider.

Kendrick worked his way around the boulders, the stable, and stood next to the rock. Hundreds of holes were visible with several large enough to hide in, or enter the cave complex. I could get lost in there without light. Maybe I can borrow a torch? How dangerous might it be to walk in? He watched the entrance from behind the bushes.

An hour passed, he decided he could blend in when the afternoon exercises were over. He would simply walk in with the group.

* * *

Quentin did not wait for the driver to open the door, but bolted from the carriage as a sailor loosened the last rope from the dock cleat. The sailor jumped and climbed the rope to the railing.

Running across the dock he was gaining on the ship. About twenty sailors had gathered along the railing cheering for Quentin. He leaped from the end of the dock. Time slowed for Quentin as he realized the rope was too far. He checked the water and saw the rope floating on the surface. Kendrick had once described looking through a tunnel when drawing an arrow. Quentin now understood, because all he could see was the brown two-inch rope.

In that instant, he hit the water. Quentin marshaled all his will to hang on. Hand over hand he pulled himself out of the water.

Red-hair shouted over the edge, "Hang on, we will pull you up!" A few seconds passed before he reached for Quentin's arms. "Nice leap."

Quentin smiled. "Thank you."

"Come with me. I will get you some dry clothes," Red-hair replied. They passed through the cabin door. "Wait here, I will return shortly."

A ball of leather fell from Oscar's coat pocket while shaking the water off. He heard Red-hair's shoes slapping in the narrow hall and shoved the leather into the pocket. After removing his wet clothes, he dressed in Red-hair's garments, removed the leather ball, and laid it out on the hammock.

It was a message from Oscar.

Quentin,

You are the King. I was proud of your new king performance at the meeting with Argo. You must use these traits in the difficult days ahead. I sense that Argo is going to detain me, if for no other reason than to weaken the government and our defenses. His pattern is to strengthen his position at every opportunity. Offering the Healing Pond hopefully will provide Kendrick time to find Althea and let you return to Manshire.

I picked the Long Bows on your protection detail because they were present on the twins rescue squad; they know where we split the twins rescue party at Dragon's Back. Find a green ribbon and take three paces south to dig up a clay pot. On the blank leather provide a brief description of our meeting with Argo. The other hide has tactics and strategy ideas for defense of Manshire. As we are uncertain of Argo's plans, we should be prepared for the worst.

See you soon,

Oscar

Quentin folded the message and stuffed it in Oscar's coat pocket. He gathered his wet clothes and returned to the main deck laying them out to dry. He napped on the deck for five hours.

A scant minute after awakening, Red-hair walked from the bridge to Quentin. "Captain Howard wishes to speak with you. Please follow me." He extended his hand. "I was impressed with your determination climbing the rope. Do not tell anyone, but I was sea sick my first year."

Red-hair held the door for Quentin. "The captain is in the middle cabin. Knock first."

"Thank you." Quentin replied.

The narrow hall was dark, lit only by the sunshine that seeped through the splintered lumber. Quentin knocked.

"Enter."

The door hinge squeaked painfully. An oil-burning lamp and one opened shutter provided the cabin's light. The room was much larger than he had anticipated. Two tilted, framed paintings signed by Bettina, Quentin's nanny, were hung on the starboard wall. Quentin quivered as he closed the door.

"I let it squeak in case I ever need a warning at night," the captain said. "Have a seat, or use the hammock, whichever you want."

"Captain Howard, you wanted to see me?"

"Yes, I am interested in how you turned out. And, I promised a good friend to pass along the information he left for you. How are you?"

"A little stressed the past six days, but I have good council."

"Challenges build your character." Howard looked about the cabin before he focused on Quentin. "Enough of that. Lieutenant Charles Cromwell, Argo's battlefield leader wanted you to know seven hundred soldiers will be transported from Cyphera to the Saraton beach. These men received archery, sword, and hand-to-hand training. Probably not a good idea to engage them with standard battle tactics, especially with your small Long Bow force."

Quentin stared out the half open window. Seven-hundred-men! Without Oscar, how am I going to win a battle with only two hundred fifty Long Bow knights? He rubbed the back of his neck with both hands, and calmly took in a deep breath of fresh sea air.

"Why are you telling me this? You were unhappy in Manshire working as the librarian," Quentin said.

"Cromwell made me promise to tell you. Also, Argo planned to kill me and burn my boat."

Quentin's eyes widened. He suddenly trusted the librarian—but not Cromwell.

"I need to thank Cromwell. But, why would he want me to know this, and lead his seven hundred soldiers against us?" It must be some kind of diversion tactic.

"Cromwell is taking care of Cromwell. He has not enlightened me concerning his plans."

"Hmmm!" Quentin stared out the half open window for a while.

"There is more," Howard said.

Quentin drew a large breath, and let it escape between his lips. "A lot more, or some more?"

He waited for Quentin to look at him. "Some. The seven hundred warriors are a backup plan."

The ship slowed. Quentin could hear the gathering of the sails. The anchor's splash preceded the tranquillity of a motionless ship. A peaceful silence was broken by the clapping of the net against the port hull and the rowboat lowered over the side.

Quentin followed Howard to the main deck.

"Be careful, and be smart," Howard said.

"Thank you for the information. Goodbye." Quentin descended the net.

"King Quentin," shouted Red-hair. "Try not to get sick this time." A burst of laughter came for the crew.

Quentin saluted them, closed his eyes, and felt the brisk wind chill his face. The Long Bows waiting on the beach gathered around a fire. But all Quentin could think about was the growing task list he must execute in the next four to eight days.

* * *

93

One of the guards delivered dinner. "Feels like a storm tonight."

"Yes, the smell is festering. I hope it does not get worse. Then there's the wind roaring over the tubes. Thank you for dinner," Althea said.

"You are welcome."

"Before you go, have you heard anything about when we are leaving?"

"Sorry, nothing yet. But, it is likely to happen at any day." He returned to his station.

A few minutes later, an argument sparked in the hallway outside the entrance to her room. It was Curtis and a voice that she could not place.

"Kendrick has died. She cannot be allowed to return to Manshire," the familiar voice said.

It cannot be true! Thoughts of her beloved's death whirled in her mind like a cold November wind whipping and mixing debris.

"I have my orders to keep her alive until Cromwell returns," Curtis said.

"Well, I am countermanding his orders."

"Seize him."

The guard's chairs chattered across the floor as they shot up to fulfill Curtis's order.

Althea felt light-headed.

A noisy scuffle ended when the familiar voice said, "Okay, okay. Can we compromise? Keep her tied up until Cromwell returns?"

The shuffling went silent.

"That we can do," Curtis replied.

The tears were streaming. He will never know he was a father. The room started to teeter-totter and spin. Her legs felt weak. Kendrick was dead!

* * *

The two guards refused to tie Althea's hands and feet. Victor glared at Curtis and his ears were turning red.

"She has not, and will not, be any trouble," Curtis said. "You two get back to guard duty. Victor, grab her hands and I will lift her feet. We can put her on the cot."

"Where can I find a rope?" Victor asked.

"You are going ahead with restraining her?"

"Yes, Kendrick's whereabouts are actually unknown. You can be certain she has escape plans, and with him outside our control she has no motivation to stay. I have been around those two long enough to know they are a strong willed pair. Hopefully, if she thinks Kendrick is dead, her escape plans will be halted." They laid her limp body on the cot. "A rope?"

"I will get one."

Disappearing Captives

She dreamed of the rose garden.

Cromwell and Althea, with the baby boy she had named Kendrick, walked between the rose bushes. Her former husband had transplanted them from his farmhouse. A dragon guided by Kendrick swooped out of the sky and removed the baby from her arms.

The dream startled her from sleep.

Pain shot through her wrist when she attempted to wipe the salt from her dried tears. She lay on the cot staring at the rope binding her hands and feet. Her energy was depleted. Everything had gone wrong—he had not escaped.

Kendrick was dead.

Quietly she cried.

Cromwell arrived fifteen minutes later. While apologizing, he removed the rope. "Victor is a head strong youngster with his own personal goals. His motives are good, but his execution is poor."

"I never liked him." She wiped her cheeks, tried to control her sniffles, but could not suppress the hiccups. Althea rubbed her scarred wrists.

Cromwell leaned back to see through the passage. His enthusiastic whisper surprised her. "I can help you escape, but we will have to go together, soon. When Argo finds out, I will be his next victim."

"What?"

"Shhh...I have always wanted to be a sailor. When the invasion begins I will leave the battle field and join Howard's crew." He glanced out the passage.

Althea stared at Cromwell then shook her head. "What are you not saying?"

He looked away. "With Kendrick gone, we could start a new life in Cyphera."

Althea was swimming in confusion, but she felt he was not being honest with her. Each thought was rapidly replaced before she could focus on Kendrick's death, the Saraton invasion, the baby, and a proposal—from a man that had been her enemy only a moment ago. Further complicating matters was his unspoken or-else clause—escape with me or take your chances here.

Althea stood and paced the chamber. She changed directions randomly. Several times she stared at Cromwell, then back to the floor.

"I have an oath to my kingdom. I must honor my commitments."

Cromwell looked down the tunnel. "What would make you reconsider?"

"We have spent maybe twenty hours together. Quite honestly, I may never remarry," Althea said. "A sailor's wife is a lonely existence because her husband is at sea most of the time." Besides, she thought of Cromwell as the head-of-the-snake—stopping him would end this conflict.

He stared at her, and then looked away. Cromwell swallowed hard and pressed his lips together. Without another word Cromwell stood striking his head on the ceiling. Stooping, and rubbing his head, he left the room with the rope.

Trying to comfort her mind, she sat on the edge of the cot staring at the floor and shaking her head.

She had two obligations left—her baby and Manshire Province. Argo was responsible for Kendrick's death, Cromwell might return with hopes of changing her mind or ending her life, particularly if she refused him again. Escape was the only option that supported her obligations.

Althea decided waiting another two hours for the guards to sleep was more risky than escaping now.

Gathering the ladle, the long candle, and four stubby candles, Althea lit all the candles and placed them in the ladle's cup, the wax drippings filling in around the long candle.

She moved to the oval side room, carefully ripping her dress into rope strips and a knapsack. Tying one end to her waist, she removed her shoes and rolled them in the knapsack. She tied the other end of the dress rope to the knapsack so it would dangle below her feet.

With the rope Althea had made from her cotton slip undergarment tied to the middle slat of the table, she slowly lowered herself into the hole. There was precious little room to maneuver; she had to be fully extended with her hands gripping the rope above her head. Repositioning the ladle with one hand while holding on to the cotton rope was extremely difficult.

When her feet touched the angled slope, she was three feet below the opening. Her breathing was erratic, and her body temperature had dropped, she was sure of it. Biting her tongue, she fought the sense of fainting. Every vital muscle was rigid—yet her hands, arms, and feet were shaking uncontrollably. *Kendrick, why did you have to die? I need your will and your skill.* She began to cry. It did not matter who heard her. *Kendrick, I need you to rescue me!*

Near panic, she frantically struggled to get back to the opening of the hole.

A small burning sensation grew with each minor upward victory. It eventually escalated into an emotional bonfire, one of rage. Anger with such intensity she had never experienced filled her being—*Cromwell lied to me, Kendrick cannot rescue me, and Oscar's protection service was completely inadequate.* Her body temperature had warmed as her wrath focused on the liar, the new void brought on by Kendrick's death, and the meager protector. At the opening, she held the rope tightly. She felt ashamed for letting her fear have control.

Slowly shaking her head she took a deep breath, then straightening herself she felt a spark of courage to try again—success would be hers. Her feet felt the wall, she gauged its size and checked for sharp points before lowering herself another four inches. Her simmering anger controlled her nausea and panic.

Althea estimated she had been in the tube thirty minutes and had traveled fifteen feet when suddenly her feet could not feel the wall. She nearly panicked. No! Control the fear. Think this through. She took a deep breath. I am entering a bigger tube or room, or I am suspended above the hot water that heats this cave. Carefully she continued—minutes later, the knapsack became weightless. Then her feet felt the knapsack—it must be on a floor, or maybe a ledge. Her shoulders, head, and arms were still in the tube. She slowly stooped to clear the low ceiling. It was dark, except for a tiny reflection. Estimating the distance to the sliver of light was impossible as everything between her and the scant light was the same black void.

The only sound came from her heart. The complete absence of a visual reference was discomforting, and chilled her. Her bonfire was dwindling. Flaming Dragons! Kendrick, I need your reassurance.

Seeking comfort, Althea licked her lower lip and played with her hair.

Althea took a deep breath and held onto the rope as she re-entered the tube for the ladle. Her shoulders were shaking, and her hungry stomach ached.

She was a foot inside the tube when suddenly the rope went slack. A few seconds later, half the broken middle slat from the table hit her head. Her mind was racing for an explanation. Have I been caught? She sensed her logic was flawed. Her mind was tired, but suddenly it became clear—It did not matter because all the men were too big to follow through the tube.

She was exhausted, her muscles ached, and a new problem: drops of blood, from the slat, ran slowly down the side of her face.

The candle illuminated only fifteen feet of the floor. She carefully set the ladle against the wall, and after that coiled the hand-made rope.

She had to sit awhile—exhaustion claimed her—she slept.

Walking through the rose garden with Kendrick and the baby filled her dreams. It was a joy. Suddenly from the sky, a dragon, with one white eye, swooped across the garden and took the baby from her arms.

Her entire body twitched causing Althea to wake abruptly. The candle burn indicated about two hours had passed since entering the hole. She had been asleep for about half that time.

Every muscle ached, but she had to press on. She looked at the target of dim light, took a deep breath, and mouthed a prayer.

Althea gathered the ladle, the knapsack, and the broken middle slat. Tossing the slat a few feet forward, she listened as it skidded across the floor. There was no splash or delayed sound of it striking the sides of a tube—she could move forward.

* * *

Holding a torch, Cromwell stood in the cave entrance hoping Althea had escaped because she could create trouble for him. He had been foolishly attracted to her, and for the first time had wanted to share a boyhood dream to be a sailor with someone. Cromwell would easily have left Argo and his plans for those bright blue eyes and that fiery spirit.

He suspected a rejection was likely, but he knew his heart would ache if she said no.

Curtis walked to the entrance next to Cromwell and informed him that shifts of twenty-five men had been ordered to patrol the giant Whistling Forest rock. "She must be hiding in one of the chambers. How did she fit through that hole?"

"Did I not warn you that she was planning an escape?" Cromwell said.

"Yes sir. We will find her. She cannot be too far with only a little more than an hour lead." Curtis scanned the dark forest. "We should have listened to Victor. Where do you think he went?"

"He is on the road to Argo, and I suspect he will be making a bid for my job." It is a grand mistake for Argo to replace the battlefield commander days before the battle, but he has a gift for making strange decisions work.

"What should we do if he continues to countermand your orders?"

"Restrain him."
Cromwell walked away.

* * *

Unable to determine how far she had traveled or how much further she had left, Althea tossed the slat piece a fourth time. At five paces the wooden piece appeared on the fringe of the candle's flame. In two steps she would stoop to toss it toward the illusive natural light.

A gust of wind whistled across the tubes and blew out the candle. Leaving her in total darkness.

Flaming Dragons!

She attempted to summon the anger that had fortified her strength in the tube, but the fire was gone. Sitting on the cool floor, chin in her palms, her mind was calm. Althea's fear of dying alone no longer scared her. Slowly she gathered the supplies, crawled toward the dim light, gently sweeping her hand to find the slat, then toss it ahead. She repeated the process until she had arrived at the reflected light.

Strangely, the blue moonlight warmed her. She closed her eyes letting the soft light bath her face with hope—she smiled.

This tube's diameter was larger than the listening hole with a minor incline to the fifty-foot tube. Hastily she tied the slip rope to the supplies and to her waist. Carefully, she crawled on her forearms. The larger tube was a blessing.

Arriving at the top opening, she discovered the reason for the faint light—the opening was covered with undergrowth. She rolled over in the tube and pulled her knapsack near. The knife she had taken from today's dinner tray lay on top of the supplies. She carefully cut the undergrowth from the opening.

Now what? She had been so concerned about escaping the 'prison' she had forgotten to plan the return to Manshire castle. She slowly lifted her head out of the hole to survey the area. There were trees and undergrowth as far as she could see on one side. Rotating halfway around, she witnessed twenty plus men carrying torches. They must be looking for her. Rotating back to the crawling position she prepared to exit the tube.

Someone tapped her shoulder.

Every muscle froze as fear shot through her body. I have been caught.

"Althea," came the soft whisper.

She was deeply confused. The voice was Kendrick's but he was dead. Could it be Kendrick's ghost?

She rotated to see Kendrick on his hands and knees.

Without thinking she reached up, holding onto Kendrick's collar, and kissed him.

"I am so happy you are not dead," she whispered. An infectious smile adorned her face, and tears streamed down her cheeks.

A quizzical expression graced his face. "No, I am very much alive, and have been hiding in the undergrowth trying to find a way in. I abandoned my plan to enter through the cave entrance when these men came out. They are looking for you."

Kendrick cast his gaze in each direction. The soldiers had dispersed. He lifted her from the hole. "Sit here for a minute so we can determine our next move."

She hugged him and whispered, "I was very angry at you earlier tonight, but the anger helped me overcome my fear."

Kendrick glanced at her and scratched the back of his head. He stared at her scratched legs, the short raggedy dress, and the dried bloodstain along her hairline. "Are you okay?"

"Yes I am fine and will explain later." She placed a hand on Kendrick for balance while she pulled on her shoes with the other hand.

"Okay, follow me. We need to borrow one of Argo's horses."

At the roped temporary stable, several minutes passed before Kendrick tugged her hand. She followed in silence. He retrieved his horse and the next one.

"You hid your horse in their stable?" she whispered.

"Sure, look around, there must be thirty horses in here."

She smiled.

As they walked out the corral, Althea asked, "Should we scatter the other horses?"

"The horses will attract attention roaming about. Everything looks normal if the horses are in the corral. The soldiers will assume we are on foot which I hope keeps them close to the cave. We will walk up the road and mount the horses after the first curve. We can get a big lead before they figure out where you are," Kendrick said.

"When will we get back to the castle?"

First, we have to take you to a safe place, then we have some digging to do."

* * *

The cloud cover blocked the moon making the ride along the trail difficult. When the moon momentarily peeked through the clouds Kendrick would smile, look to the stars, and increase speed.

For the past several hours she thought they were traveling away from Whistling Forest toward Manshire castle. But, none of the silhouettes looked familiar. She wanted to know their destination, but Althea did not want to disrupt Kendrick's concentration on the trail.

Kendrick stopped. "We will be leaving the trail and walking across some fields. Can you endure for another half hour?"

"Yes. Thank you for asking. Can you tell me what the plan is?"

"Sure. We are going to dig up a clay pot, which will tell us where Oscar and Quentin are. Then, we will decide our next steps."

"So, do we have a plan at this moment?" Althea asked.

"Yes, but I expect we will adjust it when we find the clay pot."

"Surprisingly, I am comfortable with our lack of a plan."

"Do not get attached to what seems like an absence of planning."

He looked at her grin, and smiled back, then reached for her hand.

The fields were sprouting with rows of short green plants. The moon's light reflected off the damp soil. Every five acres they had to squeeze through a hedge.

"What took you so long to find me?" she asked.

'There were no clues. You disappeared literally without a trace. And our only clue was from an old lady that we had a difficult time finding. Then the ransom letter arrived."

Althea's fingers momentarily covered her mouth. "I just remembered, Cromwell told me you are being followed. They used the threat of your death to keep me from escaping."

"That explains why I was specifically cast from the meeting." Kendrick checked the trail ahead and gently scratched his chin. "Father had kept his suspicion that Victor had a secret life until the ransom letter. We could not take a chance with your safety, so we set a trap to see if anyone followed me. I was sad when it was Victor."

"Victor showed up at the cave. He argued with the leader. I thought you had died. I fainted and awoke to bound hands and feet."

The moonlight leaked through a slit in the clouds. Kendrick stared at her wrists, lowered his eyes to her equally abraded ankles, and noticed the light twinkling off her tears. He embraced her.

Althea's world was suddenly quieter than an angel's breath. She heard only his whisper, "Forgive me Althea, I have put duty before you. Your ordeal must have been awful. It takes great courage to challenge the unknown alone." She felt his arms squeeze tighter.

With her head pressed against his chest, she felt safe.

"Thank you Kendrick." Althea closed her eyes and held him. The last thing she remembered was Kendrick saying—"I love you."

* * *

Kendrick had carried her until they arrived at the buried clay pot. He gently sat her on the ground, removed the saddle, and then placed the blanket on the ground. He moved Althea to the blanket. She woke. "Rest Althea. I am here. You are safe."

When Kendrick was certain she was asleep, it took two minutes to find the smoothed earth where he had buried it. Carefully stabbing the ground, his knife struck the clay pot. With his fingers, he removed the earth around the top. He removed the leather piece from the jar, but it was too dark to read the note.

Dawn was two hours away and the clouds blocked the moon. He rested against a tree a few paces from Althea.

Kendrick walked, checked Althea's blanket, and led the horses to grass. He was fighting sleep. Tonight, Althea could not find him sleeping. He wanted her to have confidence that he was her protector and needed to be well rested in the upcoming days.

At dawn he was reading the message on the leather piece, but before he had finished, his horse whinnied. He folded the leather and hid it inside his shirt. He shook Althea's shoulder, placed his finger over her lips, and quietly withdrew an arrow from the quiver.

Had Althea's captures followed her? Could she survive being a hostage again? The color had left her face and the silhouette of her trembling chin bolstered his determination to keep her safe and free.

A couple of minutes later two dark outlines approached. I can protect her from two soldiers. Kendrick placed an arrow in his bow. If he waited for them to get closer their silhouettes would not continue to fade into the dark background. They had not been as careful as Kendrick thought. His heart pumped harder as he thought about how easy Cromwell's men had found them.

He was prepared to let it fly when he noticed the two men had raised their hands.

"Who goes there?"

"It is the sergeant and a Long Bow."

"Approach." Kendrick stood and checked on Althea.

"How are you?"

"Much better," Kendrick said, relieved he would not have to fight.

"I want to read a note from Quentin." He waited until they were standing near. "Kendrick. Quentin here. Oscar in Venela while Argo validates the healing pond. See map below. Writing this on Saturday – six days left on Oscar's travel estimate for a round trip to the healing pond. I will be moving the ministers and most of the Long Bows. Oscar said when you rescue Althea, keep her moving and stay clear of Manshire castle. We saw several shiploads of men being transported to a beach two hours ride south of Port Welton. The former Manshire Librarian is the ship's owner, and no longer wishes to have an allegiance with Argo. However, we know that where Argo is concerned we cannot be certain the information he gave me is true. The ship's owner said it would take twelve days to transfer the full seven hundred soldiers. God's speed."

"That is the end of the note. Sergeant, you should return to Manshire to help Quentin. Althea, do you feel up to a rescue?"

Before she could answer the sergeant said, "Do you think it is wise to place her so close to Argo?"

Kendrick noticed her furrowed brow. "The last place Argo will attempt to find her is under his nose."

With a half grin and wide eyes Althea nodded to Kendrick. "Clever."

* * *

Victor arrived at Venela in the early morning after a long walk from the port. The guards walked in a pattern around the palace grounds—unusual, as they normally stood at station.

"Halt. State your name."

"Victor. I am here to see King Argo."

"Wait here. I will see if he wishes to see you."

"Tell him the queen has escaped and we do not know where her husband went."

The guard stared at Victor for several seconds before he turned toward the palace door. A few minutes later he reappeared to escort him.

Argo was eating when he entered the dining room. Victor sat on a chair near the door.

"Come, sit here." Argo pointed at a chair across the table. "Tell me the guard mis-spoke and that Althea is still in our grasp."

Victor swallowed, checked the table for a knife near Argo, then replied, "I cannot, for she has escaped. And, I was tricked to follow a man dressed like Kendrick."

Argo's cheeks and forehead turned red. As he stood quickly the chair legs rattled against the flagstone floor. Argo's pacing suddenly stopped, he grabbed the knife, and jabbed it into the tabletop between Victor's middle fingers. "How could this happen?"

With his head bowed, he remembered the rumors—he did not dare challenge Argo by looking into his eyes. "I arrived at the cave to ensure Queen Althea was in our custody. I argued with Curtis to tie her hands and feet, but he refused—he had orders from Cromwell. I tied her wrists and ankles." Argo was pacing. Victor was feeling brave and could not help himself. He lifted his head and watched Argo.

"If she was tied up, how did she escape?"

"Cromwell removed the rope. I think he is captivated by her."

Argo stopped across from Victor and gently placed his hands on the table's edge. "And, how did you lose Kendrick?"

"As I said, a Long Bow dressed like Kendrick tricked me into following the wrong man." Argo's stare intensified. The red cheeks and forehead returned. Victor thought Argo's eyes had turned red for a few seconds.

Then without any cue, Argo's natural coloring was restored, and his tenor was soothing.

"You were tricked! Hmmph. I paid you to follow a farm boy. I had you trained with my best archers and..."

Victor, wanting to take advantage of the calm Argo repeated, "But, it was not my fault."

He noticed Argo's eyes temporarily glance at something behind him. Victor wanted to check out what had caught Argo's attention, but decided he should keep an eye on the knife.

"...not your fault..." Argo whispered repeatedly as he paced. He stopped across the table and made eye contact with Victor. "I have a special assignment for you. You can restore your value to Saraton by eliminating the traitor Cromwell, Queen Althea, King Quentin, and Kendrick."

"And Oscar?"

"I have taken care of Oscar. He will not be a threat to us."

Secondary Wounds

"We are going to meet a new friend. You will like him and his wolf," Kendrick said.

"Should we travel straight away to Venela?"

"This new friend has special knowledge of Argo's palace."

"And the wolf?"

Kendrick heard the shaking in her voice and noticed she was biting her lip. He decided to lighten her mood.

"I do not think the wolf has ever been to Argo's palace."

They rode in silence until they arrived at the meadow.

"Welcome to Bernard's home. Looks like we will be waiting for a while," Kendrick said.

"How can you know that?"

"Exeter is not here to greet us."

"You said his name was Bernard." Rustling sounds came from behind Althea. She twisted in the saddle and immediately froze as a wolf sat five yards from her. She whispered, "Kendrick, the wolf is here!"

"Good, we will not have to wait." He dismounted and walked to pet Exeter.

A 'young teenage boy' wearing a monk's hat entered the clearing.

"Welcome, Kendrick. And who is this lovely lady?" Bernard asked.

"Bernard, this is Queen Althea. Althea this is Bernard Paxton."

Her head tilted slightly as she stared at the meadow. "Where have I heard the name Paxton before?"

"I am Argo's brother," Bernard replied.

"Kendrick, have you lost your mind?" she whispered, her face turning a cream color. Kendrick thought she might faint.

Bernard extended his hand to her. "Please, let me help you off your horse. I have a story for you that will explain everything. Come. You need to eat."

She looked to Kendrick who nodded. She dismounted slowly keeping Exeter in sight.

Gently, Bernard took her hand. "Your wrists. Do they hurt? I have something to treat those sores." He led her toward the cave. Exeter followed.

Althea frequently looked over her shoulder watching Exeter.

"Argo is my brother who ordered that I be left alone in the forest. His plan was for me to die. But, as you can see, his plan failed."

Bernard moved the door panel and pointed to the big rock next to the table. "Sit here, I will bandage your wrists."

Exeter's head and a paw lay on Althea's thigh. On the sixth attempt she started to pet Exeter. The wolf looked up at her.

Bernard had walked to the other side of the bed then returned with a small box. He removed a leather ball and gingerly opened the flaps. Bernard rubbed the thick, sweet smelling salve on her wrists and covered it with a strip of white cotton.

"They already feel better," Althea said.

"Let me get some clothes for you."

"No, no. You have already done more than we came here for."

Bernard leaned in toward Althea and whispered, "I get so few guests, please let me replace these rags you are wearing. We are about the same size—you are a bit taller." Bernard winked.

"Okay, it would be nice to have some clean clothes," she replied.

"Kendrick, you could use some clean clothes also. But I know you are not here for clothes, so why are you here?" Bernard asked. He opened a bag and removed a shirt and pants.

"I am again imposing on your special knowledge. This time it is the Paxton Palace in Venela."

110

"Kendrick, my friend, you are not imposing. I am happy I can help." He handed the pants to Althea. "Would you hold these up please?" Scratching his chin he inspected the pants. "Okay, can you hold this shirt now?" A few seconds passed. "Okay, I will take those." He sat on one of the bed's logs. "This will only take a few minutes. Kendrick, there is food in the basket. Please eat."

Bernard continued talking and working, "The palace is an old two story winery with a stone cellar beneath. The ground floor is the offices for Argo and staff, kitchen, dining room, and the meeting room. The second floor has eight bedrooms." Bernard held up the pants looking at Althea. "Try these on."

"The cellar is a large room with large beams resting on square columns holding the palace above," Bernard said. "It was used for storage and served as a prison on occasion. It has two entrances; one from the inside at the back of the kitchen, and a large oak door in the back wall outside."

"Well, are you two going outside?" Althea asked.

Bernard pointed toward the door as he and Kendrick went outside.

"Does the outside cellar door need a key?" Kendrick asked.

"If it does, Argo will have the key." He yelled to Althea. "Are the pants okay?"

"Yes."

"Try the shirt. It is on the edge of the table."

"Do you know how many guards?" Kendrick asked.

"During my father's time there were maybe ten. It is not a thing a boy pays attention to."

"The shirt fits well," she yelled. "You can come in now."

He removed a monk's hat from the bag of clothes, and handed it to Althea. "This will complete your disguise as a man while snooping around the palace. Let me draw the floor plan for you."

* * *

The assembly hall was arranged for a meal with three rows of tables instead of a U shape for a ministers' meeting. The low

111

drone of the conversations filled the room like smoke from a roasting pig.

Quentin counted the eleven attendees. Banging the gavel on the tabletop quickly silenced the crowd. "Take your seats. I have a few announcements." Quentin watched the ministers' heads turning to find comfort. "It is true that Althea has been rescued. The sergeant informed me this morning that she is free and safe." A cheer preceded their big smiles. "But our meeting with the new Saraton king in exile is a big concern. It is our belief that Reginald's twins were kidnapped to make way for the queen's abduction. It appears that King Argo's plans include elaborate diversions."

"If the queen is safe, why do we care about his ploys?" asked a minister.

"We boarded from a secluded beach after about fifty men left the ship. When we docked, another fifty men were ready to board. But, if our assumption is valid, these soldiers are a subterfuge meant to keep us occupied while Argo executes another plan. As the king, I have decided to take a defensive position." Quentin waited for the whispering to quiet.

"What if we think you are making a mistake?" the money minister, nearest Quentin asked.

"Mistake or not, I am the king and have plans to protect us from an engagement with Argo," Quentin replied.

"You are only the temporary king with no authority."

"Sergeant, do I have authority?"

"Yes, my king. Oscar has ordered me to follow your commands without question."

Reginald stood. "You have my support. What can I do?"

Six more ministers stood.

"To insure the stability of Manshire I am removing the ministers from the castle and holding you in the farm homes of Reginald and Oscar. Reginald will be in charge while you are separated from the castle."

"You cannot do this," the money minister said.

Quentin stared at him, "I can, and here is proof." He pointed toward a Long Bow at the door, snapped his fingers, and followed by flipping his hand toward the outspoken minister. The knight moved beside the minister. "Do you doubt my power now?"

"The sergeant will organize the Manshire Army to combat the Saraton Militia. Long Bow Knights will train our army. They will guard the castle, until, or if we need them somewhere else."

"Last item, I will deploy the Long Bows to provide maximum protection to the castle and engage the Saraton Militia, if needed."

Quentin dismissed the meeting. But, at the same time, he was very concerned that his creation of a Manshire army, not mentioned in Oscar's message, would interfere with his plans.

* * *

Arriving at Port Welton required a long day of riding. Althea and Kendrick rested outside of town. After a meal of roots and berries, he unsaddled their horses.

"We need to create a distraction away from you," Kendrick said.

"Do you have a plan, or are you actually asking my opinion?" Althea asked.

"You know me well," Kendrick said. He hesitated to consider the best words for his next remark. "I suggest you act as my squire. We can hide you under saddle blankets and weapons. No one will suspect the queen to dress and act as a squire."

Kendrick noticed the sudden break of eye contact.

"This is your best plan?" She said with a heavy sigh.

"No one will pay any attention to you as a squire. What concerns you about this scheme?"

"I am weak from captivity and escaping, and saddle weary—not sure I can carry saddles, blankets, and weapons."

"We can leave the saddles with the livery. I can carry the weapons."

"Can we decide tomorrow after hopefully a good night's rest?"

"Certainly." Kendrick decided to devise an alternative plan. He had seven hours until dawn. His initial thoughts were Fletcher,

Harker, or Butler. Kendrick's head bobbed a couple times, then he fell asleep.

His next memory was Althea shaking his shoulder. She whispered, "Kendrick it is time to find passage to Cyphera."

Daylight had filled every corner of the sky. Startled, he rose quickly. "We are late. I slept in. How are you feeling this morning?" He stretched his arms and legs.

"I feel rested," Althea said. "I may have a solution for our dilemma."

"What is your idea?"

"I can be your prisoner."

Kendrick's muscles went stiff. "That's absolutely unacceptable!" he said, though he knew the instant he finished speaking her solution was the right choice. She had the wrist scars. He would not have to worry about explaining the bandages.

He retrieved the rope tied to the saddle, and removed a small bag of coins from a secret pocket in the front seam. Althea had removed the wrist bandages. She held her wrists together, he could not look her in the eyes as he tied the rope. "Your wrists have improved." He took a deep breath. "I hate having to do this."

He helped her mount the horse, handed her the reins, and the lead rope from her wrists.

She gave him the reins and rope after he mounted his horse.

"Are you ready?" he asked.

"Yes." She lifted her wrists and pointed forward. "Proceed, we need to rescue Oscar."

They arrived at the livery stable, boarded the horses, stored the saddles, paid the blacksmith, and strolled modestly to the docks each carrying a saddle blanket. Althea also carried her escape supplies sack.

The next ship to Cyphera was scheduled to disembark in the early afternoon. After paying the shipping company clerk for two passages, Kendrick guided Althea to a shady location. He was careful to avoid comforting and waiting on her.

She glanced in each direction before asking, "What are we doing for transportation to Venela?"

"I will worry about that when we arrive."

A couple of hours passed before the clerk notified them it was time to board.

The ship was fully loaded and several nets containing freight were stored on the deck. Kendrick pulled Althea to the port side with a view of the ocean.

The ship's owner, cruising the deck, stopped in front of Kendrick. "What has this scalawag done?"

"Thief. Stole bags of money from merchants."

Kendrick glanced toward Althea—her head staring at the deck. He could feel her anger as the owner kicked her leg. "There will be no stealing on this ship or you will find the end of the plank." He turned his attention to the now standing Kendrick. "Keep him under close watch, I cannot let a thief go unpunished. I would not be able to control the crew."

"Understood." He tugged on the rope. "I will keep him on deck in full view of the crew."

"You do that." He strolled away.

When Kendrick sat, she whispered, "Remind me to revoke his access to the port. And you, can stop tugging so hard."

"I think it is best we limit our talking. Your voice might permit the owner to give us a closer look at that plank."

"Fine!" She rolled over on her side away from Kendrick. There was something different about her flat response and posture. She wrapped her arms around her legs and her chin touched her knees. Her world was reduced to a three-foot by three-foot space on the deck of a ship. As if struck by lightning, Kendrick realized Althea was back in prison with restricted movements, confined spaces, tied wrists, and no one to talk to. He turned away staring at the water feeling helpless.

After nine hours, the ship bumped the Cyphera dock. A winch and sailors began unloading a net from the deck, while several men held torches successfully challenging the darkness.

The sleep had been good for Althea. Although Kendrick had tied the rope loosely, her wrists were sore.

As Kendrick walked down the plank with Althea in tow he noticed seven single-sail fishing boats tied to the dock, a locked storage shed was the only building at the dock. The outline of a barn was difficult to make out in the distant dark.

Kendrick, with Althea in tow, approached a wagon of produce, "Can you provide us with a ride to Venela?"

"If you help us unload, and load the freight from the ship."

"Thank you," Kendrick said. He turned his attention to Althea.

"You try to escape and I may not be so accommodating next time," he added as he untied her wrists.

She placed a hand on her grumbling stomach. "When are you going to feed me?" she asked. Her hands were shaking and her red eyes were in constant motion.

"Soon."

The only item removed from the ship was a high back chair. Kendrick sat in the chair and Althea laid on the wagon's floor for the thirty-minute ride to Venela.

Waiting for the wagon to disappear, she rubbed her wrists. "Wish I had some of Bernard's ointment."

"I was thinking the same thing. We have about four hours to dawn. We can rest until then."

* * *

Alone, Quentin focused at the floor with his head in hands. A knock on the door startled him. "Yes, come in." Quentin stood.

The sergeant entered the room.

"What have you to report?" Quentin asked.

"We have captured three spies. Their stories are perhaps too similar. I suggest we jail them separately until Oscar can interrogate them. "

"Yes. How is the army training going?" Have I created the dark cloud on the horizon? Is my army decision going to interfere with Oscar's plans?

"We have gathered every man between sixteen and thirty-five. About four-hundred total." The sergeant cleared his throat. "My King Quentin, I was wondering; is it wise to remove all the able bodied man from the town?"

"We will replace some with Long Bows residing in homes. Any information from Reginald?" Quentin asked.

"A Long Bow pair returned from the farms this morning. Everything is going as well as can be expected."

"I am concerned that the center of our government is half a day's ride from the castle without protection." Quentin's hands rested on his hips as he paced. "Are the Long Bows continuing to build up at the grand curve?"

"Yes, my king." The sergeant cleared his throat. "Rest assured that the eight man patrols leave the castle, two depart to the grand curve, and only six return."

"I too am wondering how all this fits together when we are uncertain what, if anything, is going to happen. But, our confidence in Oscar's intuition and unusual methods will keep us engaged," Quentin said.

"Are you sure he is alive?"

* * *

At dawn, the bright colors of the rainbow tinted the cloud cover that had moved in overnight. Kendrick could feel the humidity when he rubbed his hands together, and hoped the rain would favor the mountains.

He checked on Althea. She was awake. "Rain?"

"Maybe...probably."

'Then we need to gather as much information as possible." She stood.

Kendrick pointed past the palace identified by the merchant last night. "I think I saw a path about a quarter mile before we left the wagon."

Kendrick hid his weapons and hat.

Carrying the wood they had gathered up the inclined road they passed the gated entrance to the palace grounds and counted the guards.

They continued past the palace until Kendrick pointed to the path. He left the road and maneuvered between the overgrown grape vines. Ten feet into the vineyard Kendrick and Althea left the firewood.

"It appears the rows continue around the palace. Try to avoid dried leaves and twigs."

Kendrick led the way through the rows until he had a full view of the back of the palace. A thirty-foot wide stone patio extended from the stairs on the right to the retaining wall on the left. The vegetation was cut back about ten feet from the patio's edge. The barren area was littered with several burned branches. The weathered oak door had turned grey and grain-less from lack of care. The grain was visible in the newer timber crossbars.

"The cellar door is oak. From the rust on the lock and use of two timber crossbars, it appears they do not use a key," he whispered. "We will watch the guard movement until we know their marching patterns. Then, I will enter through the cellar. Early afternoon should be a good time to pass through the kitchen."

"I have not seen a guard with more than a spear, sword, and knife—none have arrows," she said.

Mid-morning, Althea tapped Kendrick's shoulder then pointed toward the palace. A well-dressed young man walked down the patio stairs followed by three guards—two carrying smoldering branches and one carrying a torch. The guard handed the torch to a branch wielding guard while removing the timber crossbars.

A few minutes later Althea and Kendrick heard muffled screaming. He was about to bolt out of the vineyard when she placed her hand on his shoulder. "We only have knives, we are no match for their spears and swords."

Flaming Dragons.

The young man walked onto the patio followed by three guards. He slapped the second guard before yelling a few inches from his face. "Once again you have applied too much pain. We cannot get information from him if he passes out."

"That must be Argo," Althea whispered. "Only a king could slap a guard and live."

They watched in horror as Argo quickly pulled the sword of the guard near him and stabbed the second guard. "Take him out of my sight. The head cook can care for him in the barn. Secure the door before you go." He abruptly turned and shuffled up the stairs.

A couple of minutes after the guards were gone Kendrick said, "I might need a diversion to get through the kitchen or upstairs. Are you prepared to scream or beat on a log a few times?"

"What do you have in mind?"

"I will circle my hand near my head if I need a diversion."

"I would be happy to help."

Kendrick moved slowly toward the door. On the patio he saw the blood trail. He removed the crossbars and slowly opened the door. The room was filled with various wooden crates, a throne, chairs, and woodcarvings. The stairway at the far end was sealed. In that instant, he heard what sounded like a chain being dragged across the floor. From the doorway he saw three bloody footprints.

Four spears rested in a corner. Kendrick selected one and moved along the wall opposite the chain sound. He heard heavy breathing as he passed by the largest crate.

"Who are you?" Kendrick asked softly into the dark.

"Kendrick?"

"Father?"

"I am shackled to the wall. The keys are hanging on the boards blocking the other entrance."

Kendrick noticed the strain in Oscar's voice. "Are you okay?"

"No. My feet are burned." Oscar's voice was weak. "They tortured me for information about our military, and to keep me from running away. You need to hurry. They could return at any minute."

Kendrick felt the raw bleeding skin when he unlocked the wrist shackle. He leaned forward and lifted Oscar onto his shoulder. When he reached the door he leaned Oscar against the wall.

Kendrick slowly stretched his head out the doorframe to check if it was safe, then circled his hand above his head, twice. He watched Althea move toward the old barn on the east end of the palace grounds. Alternately, he watched for guards.

"Kendrick, where are your weapons?" Oscar asked.

"Hidden in some bushes across the road."

From the east a scream focused the guards' attention. Kendrick quietly crawled up the stairs—the guards had gathered into small groups facing the scream. A couple alternately looked between the direction of the scream and a second floor window. Kendrick assumed they sought re-assurance to enter the wooded area.

Kendrick hauled Oscar outside before replacing the crossbars.

"Good thinking," Oscar said weakly.

A second scream signaled Kendrick. He lifted Oscar then carried him into the un-kept grapevines not concerned about the sound from crushing leaves and snapping branches. He set Oscar down when they were deep in the musty vineyard.

A couple quiet minutes later, Althea surprised Kendrick when she gasped at Oscar's feet.

"I brought your weapons," Althea said.

"Thank you. Very thoughtful," Kendrick breathed. "Father, are there horses close by?"

"Yes, two carriage horses in the barn."

"Kendrick, I noticed the back of the barn is poorly maintained. We might be able to remove some of the siding. Perhaps exit out the back also," Althea said. "Let me suggest that I watch for the guards, after we move Oscar to the barn, and begin opening a hole."

"Good idea."

It took six minutes to arrive at the barn. He placed Oscar on the ground then inspected the barn for a weak spot to begin removing the wall. Picking the plaster from the wall got easier with each chunk that flaked off.

"I hear some activity." Althea looked around the corner of the barn. "We have to expedite our plan. I see Argo walking toward the stairs with three guards."

Kendrick increased the force used to remove the plaster. When the hole was big enough, Kendrick squeezed through.

The stabbed guard's eyes opened before Kendrick gently placed a saddle blanket on him. Kendrick smiled.

Kendrick returned to push chunks of plaster onto the ground. After walking the horses out the door-sized hole, he lifted Oscar onto a horse, and handed him a shirt he picked up in the barn. "We can make bandages at the port."

Kendrick rode the other horse with Althea. After clearing the aging vineyard they turned left and rode the horses past the palace gate at full speed.

Twenty minutes later they arrived at the dock. Kendrick carried Oscar to one of the fishing boats. Oscar rowed for five minutes then Kendrick unfurled the small triangular sail.

Boats & Ships

A peaceful sail through the night was one blessing for which Althea was silently thankful. On previous days she had found a few moments alone to expel the contents of her stomach. But this morning there would not be a private moment.

The little fishing boat moved in unison with the swelling waves. And the darkening skies advanced toward the small craft.

Concentrating on their situation proved to be more difficult than she had previously thought. Althea tried counting the large waves. On the twenty-third wave, she could not hold it any longer.

She doubled over holding her stomach. "Are you okay?" Kendrick asked rubbing her shoulders. She has exhausted her body with the escape from the cave, riding to Bernard's, and Oscar's rescue. And, she was sick before the kidnapping, Kendrick recalled.

"Thank you Kendrick, I will be okay. Just a little sea sick," she replied. Throughout the morning, she twisted her body several times to check the storm's progress. Each time, her complexion approached a lighter shade of anemic.

"Kendrick, grab an oar. We have to try reducing our exposure to these increasing waves and attempt to outrun the storm," Oscar said.

After thirty-three waves, Oscar's feeble effort concerned Althea. The torture, lack of food, and sleepless nights had finally crushed his energy. "Oscar, trade places with me. I will row for a while so you can rest."

"No, my queen." Looking at her stomach, his narrowed eyes gave the impression of questioning, are you sure? After shaking his head slightly for a few seconds, he straightened his back and chin before he said, "I am responsible for the circumstance we are in.

Had I expanded your protection, you would not have been kidnapped."

Kendrick stopped rowing. Althea could see his shining eyes. He rubbed both hands across his hair then took a deep breath as he leaned forward. "That's why you did not cross-examine me for the ambush!"

"How could I?"

"Father, we are participants in Althea's kidnapping. She could have ordered additional protection. I should have stayed to protect her when the twins were abducted—perhaps the four knights would not have died...Father, sit by Althea. You can take my place when I need rest."

"Son, you remind me of your mother, she saw the world differently in a very constructive way." Oscar hugged his son. "Okay my queen, I will rest."

Oscar crouched as he crossed the small craft to sit by Althea. She slid to her side at the instant a wave knocked Oscar into the water. Althea was slapped against the bottom of the boat. She rubbed her head hoping to reduce the pain. The full force of the wave had pinned Kendrick against the gunwale.

Kendrick sat up and shook his head, slinging water from his hair. He removed the oar from the lock, and extended it over the side. "Father, grab this!"

From Oscar's grimace she knew the salt water was stinging his burned feet. She gripped Kendrick's belt to keep him from being the next splash victim.

He pulled the oar until Oscar reached for Kendrick's hand. Althea took the oar. "Hold–on, another wave is about to strike." Oscar grabbed Kendrick's forearms and Kendrick, Oscar's.

When Oscar's shoulders were inside the boat's frame, he held himself in place. Kendrick then reached into the water and pulled Oscar up by his belt.

Kendrick took his place behind the oars.

Althea turned to check on the waves. "Row!" a wide eyed Althea ordered.

Oscar pointed off starboard. "Look. Land. Kendrick, drag your left oar."

The third wave raised the water to the bottom of the center seat plank and the sail's rents ripped another four inches further reducing the area for the wind to push.

"Another wave will sink the boat," Oscar said. "We are far from shore." He took the torn shirt bandages from his feet and tied them to his belt. He patted his thighs with his hands, and watched the waves.

"Prepare to swim," Kendrick said.

The ocean engulfed the boat. Peacefully the boat sank, leaving them to tread water. Althea saw the conflict in Kendrick's narrowed eyes. "If you plan on making shore you have to let them go."

Kendrick stuffed the knife into his shirt and released his weapons, watching their slow tumble through the dark water.

Althea swam between Oscar and Kendrick. Every tenth stroke Kendrick checked on them.

Part way to shore Althea stopped swimming.

"I do not think I can make it."

Kendrick slipped an arm under her shoulder. "Lie back and kick. You okay, Father?"

"I will make it."

In the water for ten minutes, Althea thought they had been swimming in place. Swimming from the wave's crest to the trough they moved closer to shore. They were exhausted when they reached the wave's lowest point. There was little swimming as they struggled to stay afloat with the under currents rising from the trough. At the wave's top, rain pushed around in the strong winds pelted them. There was precious, little time to rest.

Watching Kendrick, she saw his face twitch with every leg kick.

Ten minutes later, Kendrick felt sand. He stood in waist high water.

"We can walk to shore from here," he said. They leaned on each other trudging through the water. Twice, waves forced them to their knees. The rain had hardened the beach and continued to chill them as they rested against the grassy bank where they collapsed.

After three hours, Oscar woke Kendrick and Althea. "We need to find shelter." He looked around the trees and shore. "I recognize this place. It is the beach where we met the ship transporting us to Cyphera. That first group of warriors camped over-there."

"Look farther up the beach in the trees, there is maybe fifty campfires," Kendrick said.

A sigh accompanied Oscar's slumped shoulders when he realized a fire would not be drying their clothes. Shivers progressed up his spine from thoughts of perhaps being a prisoner again after a day of freedom.

"That could be Argo's Saraton Militia," Oscar said.

"I did not see the fires before."

"Nor I."

"Is that a ship anchored out there?" Althea asked pointing toward the west.

"I think it is. We should get moving before we are caught. There are more soldiers that I expected. We could be in trouble. Kendrick, are you strong enough to do some spying?"

"Certainly."

"Be aware around you. More soldiers might be disembarking from the ship when the waves calm. There are probably sentries. We will meet you five miles due north."

* * *

Kendrick crawled slowly on his belly through the mud and the drenched waist high grass with only his knife. He had stopped and listened at the previous five clumps of willows. He was close to a fire warming nine men and wanted to accompany them long enough to stop his cold rain induced shaking.

He counted seventy-two fires roughly six hundred fifty men. If this is a militia, where are their weapons?

Several boats from the ship loaded with men rowed in the bumpy water.

Victor followed a sneezing man wandering through the campfire hamlets. The men stood when the sneezing man joined the groups. Kendrick watched until the rowboats stopped traveling to the beach.

He spotted seven wagons covered with blankets.

Kendrick waited for the ship to leave, before walking, hunched over, along the three-foot grassy ledge toward the wagons. There were no sentries or guards around the camp or the poorly organized ramshackle wagons.

There were no tracks on the beach and no mud on the wheels. But, they could have been washed with the rain. One wheel on the third wagon was broken making it unusable. Two were missing the tongue. The trampled grass around the wagons led Kendrick to believe they were carried there with no plans to move them.

Carefully, he checked the contents of the wagons; bows, arrows, knives, blankets, shields, and swords. With fifty Long Bows I could capture the entire militia.

He was crawling to the sixth wagon when seven soldiers, the sneezing man, and Victor walked toward the last wagon.

Quickly, Kendrick collected the two bows and quivers he had appropriated, and quietly hid in the willows near the second wagon.

"All the men are now here. When the rain stops we will pass out the blankets and weapons," said the sneezing man. "Achoo! I hate spring... Each of you collect your weapons and guard the wagons. I will send twenty-five soldiers to collect their weapons and patrol the perimeter."

The seven guards removed a sword from the last wagon. Kendrick slid out of the willows like a snake.

* * *

Limping slowly, Oscar left bloody footprints on the pine needles, leaves, and spring grass. His feet would surely hamper their ability to hide quickly while traveling on known trails— wisely; he had taken a course through the forest.

Even for Althea the pace was slow, but she walked behind him to avoid pushing him beyond his foot limitations.

"I suggest we stop and let you make some clever foot protection device," Althea said.

"We must push on. The Saraton militia is larger than I anticipated. We are not prepared for any fighting force that is three or four times our size. I wish we had horses," Oscar replied.

Althea stopped frequently to check for Kendrick. It had been more than five hours since leaving the beach. Toying with her hair between taking deep breaths calmed her and kept her from running into Oscar.

Occasionally, he would stop and check on Althea. Her hands pushed on the small of her back while she moved her head from side to side. Twice she let Oscar walk ahead hoping he could not see her massaging her feet.

"We have traveled about five miles and can wait for Kendrick. My feet feel like I am walking on an anthill. And, they could use the rest."

"Do we need to worry about the militia finding us?" Althea asked, staring back at the trail.

"Before turning north, they will march east to stay on flat land." To comfort Althea, Oscar said, "He will be safe. Try to sleep."

She woke and found Oscar watching for Kendrick. "How long have we slept?"

"You, about four hours. Me, about an hour." He bit the inside of his cheek, and stared at the top of the trees.

"What is it that you want to say?"

"Are you pregnant?"

"Yes, about three months." Anticipating his next question, Althea said, "I decided to tell him later—he does not need the added distraction."

Oscar rubbed the muscles between his shoulders at the base of his neck. "You could be underestimating his reaction."

"He does not need to be worried that I might lose the baby." She looked away. "Any sign of him?"

"No, I am worried. He should have been here hours ago." Oscar turned toward her. "Night travel can be difficult with a storm blocking the moon. We will give him two more hours; then we are obligated to go. People are waiting for us at the grand curve."

Althea noticed his wrinkled brow and ashen face. His eyes revealed a father's concern, a worried Captain, and an exhausted friend. When he returned to watching for Kendrick, a hand might have wiped a tear across his cheek.

The two hours passed slowly with no sign of Kendrick.

"We must go, Queen Althea."

They had walked about half a mile when unexpectedly she heard branches cracking, horses snorting.

Oscar looked at her, pointed three fingers at the sound, and gestured to hide—his eyes, wide and alert.

He picked-up a large crooked stick, a hand sized stone, and limped to a thick trunked tree. With his back pressed against the bark he was prepared to attack to either side.

A bird whistle pierced the cold, sharp air. Oscar lowered the stick and repeated the whistle.

After a few seconds, Kendrick appeared with two rabbits draped over his shoulder and holding the reins of three horses.

Althea ran to him. They hugged in silence.

Walking with Kendrick, Althea said, "I was concerned you were caught or could not find us."

"It was a short run to Port Welton. I woke the blacksmith and offered a nice tip for our horses and tack, and purchased another horse," Kendrick replied.

"Your father's feet are getting worse."

"The healing pond is too far. Do you know how to find Bernard's cave?" Kendrick asked Althea.

"Yes. It would delay us, but his feet need treatment," Althea replied.

"Just put me on a horse so we can move faster," Oscar said. "We need to get to the grand curve."

"Do I have to order you to keep your feet from infection?" Queen Althea asked.

Oscar's tapped his fingers on his thigh. He shook his head and changed subjects. "Kendrick, what did you find out?"

"Roughly calculating, there were about six hundred fifty soldiers. An hour after you left, fifty more joined them. They had seven broken wagons storing weapons. That's where I picked-up these bows and quivers. Victor was present, following a man with one white eye who sneezed a bit. They started passing out the weapons as I left."

"The sneezing man, did you say one white eye?"

"Yes. You know him?"

"He is Cromwell—my kidnapper, and Argo's field commander—the head of the snake."

"He was standing in the cave opening after you escaped?"

"That is him."

"Kendrick, my sense is that Argo's Saraton Militia is one of his diversions. I believe he made a point of transporting soldiers for us to witness—wanting us to focus on the militia. Do you think you could stay back and find out what Argo's militia is up to?" Oscar asked.

"Certainly," replied Kendrick.

"Althea thinks the personnel at the cave were preparing a surprise attack."

"Somewhere in Saraton?"

"Not sure," Althea replied.

"We should expand our thinking. It could be an attack in Manshire; our harbor, the castle, or northern farming region. It could be the hunting lodge—Argo made a point of mentioning it. We might have to allow the Saraton locations to fall so we can protect Manshire," Oscar said. "Son, is it possible to search the area between here and the grand curve in five days?"

"It is a bit of a stretch, but if you stop to care for your feet, I'll meet you in five days."

"Good. I will go with Althea to meet this Bernard," Oscar said, mad he could not go directly to the grand curve.

"I need to start. Be careful, you are not safe until this is over—whatever this turns out to be." He kissed Althea. She held onto him for a few extra moments.

Before Kendrick had disappeared into the dark, Oscar and Althea mounted the horses. Althea led the way.

"We will ride until you want to rest, and then finish traveling to Bernard's," Oscar said.

"Then our next stop will be Bernard's."

Two Liars & A Farmer

Light leaking through the storm's tailing clouds briefly shone on the trail, enough for Kendrick to risk a hurried ride to the Whistling Forest cave. Kendrick stopped at a stream to water his horse and let it feed on the fresh spring grass.

Back on the trail he was refreshed—plans were meshing, they knew the enemy, Kendrick was gathering information on troop movement, and soon Oscar would be guiding the Long Bows.

Arriving at Whistling Forest, the early morning sun peaked above the eastern horizon. He left his horse and walked the last quarter mile. Crawling on his stomach the last fifty feet to the lookout point, he was surprised and concerned—the cave had been abandoned.

He slid down the gravel beneath the lookout point to where the rockslide met the trail to the cave opening. It was covered with tracks pockmarked by sprinkling rain. Kendrick was glad Whistling Forest had been on the very edge of the storm. Whole footprints covered partial footprints all going in the same direction.

Morning tracking was tricky because the sun created long shadows. He walked north until he found where the entire company had entered the trail. Occasionally, an undisturbed horseshoe track could be found along the edges of the footprints.

For three hours he alternated between walking the horse, trotting, and galloping until he heard the sound of many feet. He stopped to determine how close he was to the marching men. A sly smile wrinkled the corners of his mouth. Kendrick dismounted and walked his horse a safe distance from the marching men.

In that instant, the now silent forest had changed from friend to enemy—it would be his movements alerting the soldiers. Had they heard him over their marching?

"We will rest here until night," came the command followed by what sounded like extra-large rats scurrying through the underbrush.

He slipped into the forest and gently moved toward the soldiers until he arrived at the edge of a large meadow, and the oddest scene—soldiers sleeping midday. Some had covered their heads with a blanket, others rested on blankets, and some did not sleep. The horses were tied on both sides of a length of rope spanning thirty feet between two trees. Kendrick counted five sentries walking around the sleeping men.

At a safe distance, Kendrick moved through the forest slowly until he arrived where one sentry guarded the horses and three soldiers were talking—actually one did the talking and two nodded their heads. Kendrick removed his hat, crouched over, moved toward the line of horses, and wedged between a pair. But, was able to hear only parts of the conversation

"Inform   Cromwell...in   position...six   nights. Squad...two...him   in   three   days...questions...ride   straight through...now."

Hope my legs blend in. A minute later, the two soldiers rode by his temporary hideout. Kendrick disappeared into the forest leaving no trace of his eavesdropping. For twenty minutes, he circled around the encampment until he found the road. He sprinted toward his horse hoping he had not lost the opportunity to follow the two soldiers.

* * *

In the saddle, Althea struggled to keep her head up. She caught herself dozing off three times. She exercised her authority by ignoring Oscar's insistence that she stop to rest—wanting him to get care for his feet.

The trail looked familiar and she was certain they were close to Bernard and Exeter.

By late afternoon she stopped by the meadow with the clear pond.

"Where are we?" Oscar asked.

"We are at Bernard's 'home'." She pointed to the cave across the meadow. Althea stared at the cave then twisted in her saddle. "I do not see him. We can rest here until he returns." She walked to a tree, sat, leaning back to sleep. Oscar limped to a tree near her.

Three minutes later, Oscar stood quickly. Retrieving an arrow from the quiver startled Althea. She heard him whisper, "My feet really hurt." He had placed the arrow atop the string's knot, and drawn it to his cheek—obviously waiting for the rustling noise to reveal itself.

"I should remind you that Bernard has a pet wolf. Quite friendly." The words had barely left her lips when Exeter appeared from behind Oscar while Bernard, with his hands held high, walked out of the forest toward Oscar. She remembered experiencing the same quick greeting when she was with Kendrick. Their wait had been short before Bernard and Exeter had appeared from different directions.

"Oscar, it is Bernard," Althea said quickly, hoping she was fast enough to stop Oscar.

He lowered the bow slowly.

Bernard lowered his arms. "Hello, Queen Althea. I see the clothes are holding up." He extended his hand to Oscar. "I am guessing you are Kendrick's father. I should thank you for saving my life."

Exeter placed his wet nose against Oscar's left hand. He flinched, and his heart beat rapidly. When he glanced at Althea, she winked. His heartbeat slowed. "Pardon? Have we met?"

"I received a copy of your book along time ago. It has been my guide to survival."

"Happy to help, I think." Oscar scratched the back of his neck.

Bernard looked at the bloody rags tied around Oscar's feet. "Oh my goodness, what happened here?"

"Argo tortured him for military information, and to keep him from running away," Althea replied. "Can you do for his feet what you did for my wrists?"

"Let me take a look. This way." Bernard pointed to the cave.

When they arrived at the cave, Bernard instructed Oscar to sit on the table and rest his feet on the rock. Oscar removed the bandages.

Bernard lifted a foot and his eyes opened wide along with his mouth. "I have seen this before, but not this bad."

He clinched his jaw when Bernard touched a bright red sore on Oscar's heel. Althea suspected dirt had worked through the tattered bandages.

"I can help you, but it will be painful. I will have to scrape the scabs to keep your feet from deforming. Can you stay off them for a couple days?"

Althea knew the answer. The fate of Manshire was at stake. Oscar would not let his feet interfere with his duty.

"Yes," Oscar replied.

"What?" Althea swiftly covered her mouth, but it was too late. She squeezed her eyes shut. "Flaming Dragons! I apologize." She opened her eyes and glanced at Oscar. "I was so shocked by your response. But I should have realized your decision would be what is best for Manshire."

"It is not ideal, but I can stay on a horse for a few days," Oscar said.

"Clever," Bernard added quietly.

"Have you treated burns like these before?" Oscar asked.

He sat, removed his right boot and sock—showed his disfigured sole. "No. But I saw it done when I was an unwilling spy for Argo." Bernard slipped his sock and boot on his foot. "Before you turn down my offer, you should know you will die in the next four to six days from infection. Frankly Oscar, your chance of surviving the treatment are much higher."

Althea was pacing. Die in the next four days...chance of surviving...militia larger than anticipated...people waiting at the grand curve. Oscar was the central figure controlling the Long Bows, which had become drastically undermanned with

Kendrick's spy information. Oscar had been with her since birth keeping her safe until the recent kidnapping; however, he had managed to extend her life by manipulating Argo. While in custody, deep in her heart, she knew Oscar and Kendrick would be working on her rescue. The silence caught her attention. "What are we to do if you die?"

"Kendrick is quite capable of leading the Long Bows. He may make a few errors, but he recovers quickly from his mistakes."

"We should get these feet treated as soon as possible," Bernard said.

"Yes," Oscar replied.

Althea nodded.

"Oscar, come and lay on the bed with your feet hanging over the log. If you pass out, we will not have to worry about moving you.

While Oscar hobbled to the bed, Althea watched Bernard retrieve the box with the ointment ball. He handed Oscar a jug. "Drink enough to be happy, but not enough to sleep." Bernard heated his knife over the fire. "Let me know when you are ready."

"What is this drink? It is sweet and does not have a liqueur burn," Oscar said.

"It is a mixture of roots, flowers, honey, and berries."

Fifteen minutes later, Oscar slurred, "I am happy."

Althea cooled Oscar's face with water from the clear pond and watched a focused Bernard gently scrape the scabs from Oscar's feet. She turned her head when the mixed aromas of the drink on Oscar's breath, the decaying burned flesh, and the ointment made her nauseous.

When Bernard had heated the knife to cut away the festered flesh, Althea handed Oscar a finger thick stick to bite and a stone to squeeze for each hand. The stick did little to muffle Oscar's scream, but kept him from losing teeth. Holding his legs required her full effort.

After a painful episode, Bernard waited for Oscar's breathing to calm. He used the time to wipe the sweat from his own forehead, and dabbed the blood with a rag. The combination of Bernard whispering "good" and smiling each time upset the fidgeting Althea. She wiped the tears flowing past Oscar's ears.

Bernard gently opened the leather piece containing the ointment, then tore some clothes into bandages. "Althea, you should do this. He will need someone to treat his feet for a few days."

She knelt by Oscar, but did not look initially at his feet. A voice whispered in her head, you planned an escaped through a narrow rock tube and a large cavernous room in total darkness. This, you can do.

"Wipe a thin layer of the ointment on the wound. Let it set for a few minutes, then cover it with a fresh bandage."

Oscar snored.

"If you would like to rest, I made a spot in the meadow for you. He will sleep for several hours. I will find us some food."

Althea was dreaming within a few minutes.

She walked and Oscar limped through the rose garden. The roses were in full bloom and the fragrance reminded her of Kendrick's work tending the garden for her to enjoy. In a basket she carried a baby boy named Kendrick. The smoke from the kitchen hinted that a rare meal of grouse was being prepared. When she sat the basket down, Cromwell leaped from the cover of the rose bushes, grabbed the basket, and ran toward the marsh. Exeter leaped at Cromwell separating the basket from his hand. Bernard carried the basket back to Althea. The baby was missing.

Startled by the dream she awoke to the smell of roasted grouse. She could hear them talking. The sun was setting as she entered the cave to find Oscar leaning on his elbows. Bernard was preparing dinner.

"That is quite a remarkable shot, killing a grouse with a knife," Oscar said, dangling his feet over the end of the bed.

"I've had lots of practice. The secret is to approach them from behind. As you know they are very skittish, and take flight at the least bit of motion." Bernard turned the grouse.

"How are the feet?" Althea asked.

"They feel much better, but my head is throbbing."

"It will wear off after a good meal," Bernard added. "In another half hour the bird will be ready. Althea, can you tend the grouse while I gather a few roots?"

"Happy to help."

Oscar rubbed his temples with the heel of his hands. After a few minutes he said to Althea, "For someone that had to fend for himself at an early age, Bernard is an unusually gifted individual. His skills are well developed, my feet are unbelievably better, and he killed a grouse with a knife—which is near impossible."

"I have noticed that he always seems to be prepared to help. He did minor alterations on these clothes last time we visited and they fit perfectly. He treated my wrists, and like your feet they felt much better in just a few hours..."

Exeter walked by the opening.

"It's like he is a ghost," Althea said in a rushed whisper.

A few seconds later, Bernard entered with an armful of washed and trimmed sweet roots that he placed on the table. He poked the tip of his knife into the grouse and a drop of fat oozed out. "I think it is ready. Ladies first. Althea, would you like a leg?"

"That would be wonderful."

Bernard pulled the leg away from the bird then cut it off. He placed it on a flagstone.

"Oscar, the other leg?"

"Thank you. And a few of those roots, please."

Bernard removed the leg, and placed it on another flagstone with a few roots before handing it to Oscar.

He then removed the wings for himself.

"Tomorrow, I must leave early to tend a couple gardens, or lose the carrots and potatoes growing there. My apologizes, but I must take care of this or go hungry next winter."

"Thank you for your hospitality and doctor services. We are very grateful," Althea said.

"I must agree. You have been a lifesaver. Can we do anything for you?" Oscar asked.

"No, thank you. Stop in anytime. Remember to change the bandages every day until the redness disappears. Keep your feet out of the dirt."

The following morning, their saddled horses were tied beside the entrance, and Bernard was gone. The little box containing the ointment ball was sitting on the table along with a bag of grouse pieces, roots, and Oscar's book with a note 'For Kendrick'.

* * *

Quentin's sleep habits had vanished several days ago when he had read Oscar's leather message. It was the moment he realized his role, temporary or permanent, was not over and still vital to defending his country. Oh, how he hoped being the king was a brief duty.

He heard the bell's single chime. The army would be gathering for drills.

The army had become his major source of sleepless nights. He had a sense of Oscar's plans from the second message in the buried jar, and they did not include four hundred men being removed from their homes to battle a militia of seven hundred.

He walked to the window and opened the shutters. The army was beginning to amass, and the Long Bows separated the men into groups for training.

Three weeks ago he had been a priest. Today he was a king—an unprepared king making bold decisions on little more than a couple of boats carrying men, an insane enemy leader, and a message from Oscar whom he had not heard from in days.

The second chime interrupted Quentin's concentration, as it had done every morning.

He knelt and prayed as the sun began the day and warmed his face.

* * *

The two soldiers riding throughout the night shortened a two-day ride to a single long day. They changed their speed many times, Kendrick assumed, to protect the horses from exhaustion.

Twice he nearly revealed his position—once at sunset and then again at dawn. Both times Kendrick was distracted trying to interpret the missing portions of the orders given to the two soldiers he was following.

In position something six nights—maybe an assignment for six knights? Could be a place six nights away, or the travel time from some number to six nights. If they travelled at their current pace, it was four days to the King's hunting lodge, five days to Manshire harbor, seven days to the castle, and eight days to the farming region. Could spies have found out about the minister's secret location, or perhaps the grand curve?

Squads something two something him in three days—probably a squad identified by number two. "Him" likely refers to Cromwell. What could "in three days" mean—three days to a meeting, a first attack, or a destination?

As a precaution Kendrick kept his distance, resting his horse for twenty minutes, he then tracked the soldiers.

Five hours later while checking the ground for tracks he heard the distant sound of several horses galloping toward him. He dismounted and led his horse into the forest. The galloping grew louder. Kendrick forced his horse to the ground, laying his body over the mane, his pant legs soaking water from the wet leaves. Seconds later three men raced by. That was close.

When he stood, the horse also got up. He wiped the forest debris from his clothes. He planned to verify that the three riders had come from the enemy's militia. He took three steps when another chorus of galloping horses approached. Again he forced his horse to lie down. Four men rapidly rode passed. Kendrick knew two of them—Victor and Cromwell.

* * *

It had been two long days in the saddle—up before dawn, eating food from Bernard's bag, resting the horses for only five minutes twice a day, and riding past the sunset. The sun would set in less than an hour.

"Many of the landmarks looked familiar until a few minutes ago," Althea said. "But I am not familiar with where we are now."

"You have probably never used the north-eastern entrance to the grand curve," Oscar replied.

Five hours before midnight, about one hundred fifty Long Bows could be found napping, target practicing, wrestling, or eating. All activity suddenly stopped and a cheer followed when Oscar entered with Althea.

"You can dip your feet in the water while I catch up with the Long Bows." Oscar said.

He rode the horse toward the center of activities. "Who is in charge?"

"I am, sir," Zachary said. He was the fourth oldest Long Bow and a trusted friend, and the reason he was chosen by the sergeant. He was an average man with a big heart, fierce loyalty, and a larger determination.

"Zachary, bring me up to date."

Aware of Oscar's preferences, Zachary provided him with a general summary of the situation—after, Oscar would ask the detail questions. "Well sir, a hundred Long Bows wait at the castle, fifty in defensive positions, and fifty hidden in homes. Three spies, with one story, have been captured. And, the army continues to train."

"Army?"

"Yes sir. King Quentin commissioned an army. About hour hundred men, but we are not sure why. The Long Bows can handle any armed force from Saraton."

"Zachary, the Saraton Militia is seven hundred men that we know about, and we are sure there is at least a hundred more." A couple of whistles acknowledged the surprise. The knights looked to each other for confirmation.

"Take six knights and bring the spies here for me to interrogate. Leave and return tonight. Bind their hands and blindfold them. Have the sergeant come back with you. And mention to King Quentin that it was a wonderful surprise to find we have an army."

"Consider it done. Nice to have you back."

"Thank you." Oscar pointed at four knights. "Post two guards at the two entrances."

Oscar rode his horse to Althea. He was physically tired, but his mind had a purpose. At the grand curve he could make a difference and save his country. This was a magical location. The sparse forest, green short grass, red rock overhang, cool stream, and the gentle breeze—alone these features were nice, but the combination had a powerful calming effect."

"How is the water?"

"Wonderful. It has been a while since my last visit. I had forgotten how calming this place could be—the trees, grass, stream, breeze, and memories of clandestine meetings with Kendrick."

"We have three spies in custody. After we interrogate them, and Kendrick arrives, we can revise our plans to defend Manshire, and maybe retain Saraton."

"I heard we have an army," Althea said.

"Yes. A very nice surprise," Oscar replied. "Is it time to change the bandages? I would like to rest until the spies arrive, after that I will be on the horse for a while."

It was a five hour round trip between the castle and the grand curve—enough time to think about his interrogation technique. Three spies with one story? Another Argo scheme? He must determine if they had a prepared story or if it was coincidently the truth. And, he had to gather information on what the Saraton King had planned so Manshire could appear to be falling into Argo's trap.

The three spies arrived at the grand curve blindfolded and hands bound. Each uniquely exhibiting fear. One was clinching his jaw and jerking away from restraint. Another stood tall, but his knees shook. The last spy slumped over and made no effort to hide his nervousness.

Oscar glanced to a trio of Long Bows standing behind him. Their nod told him they were ready.

Long Bows escorted the spies, as instructed by the Captain, helped the trio off the horses, sat them together, and kept them informed.

"Good morning. Well it is good at this moment, but in an hour only one of you will be enjoying the rest of the day. Here is what you can expect from us—every effort to arrive at the truth. You can save yourself a lot of pain by telling us what you know. First we will test you with what we know based on information from our spies." Their heads looked up at him though they were blindfolded.

He moved his horse closer to them. "One of you might survive the day relatively unharmed, and two of you will greatly suffer or perhaps die." The trio's reaction was instantaneous as they moved their heads toward his voice. It was probably a good turn of events that he was interrogating from a horse. "Okay, separate them."

Each Long Bow escort kept his spy informed on the terrain. When Oscar was comfortable with the spacing, he lifted his arm and waved his hand to sit them. The other Long Bows sat or knelt in silence to watch Oscar.

Oscar moved to the spy on the left. He was short with broad shoulders and his hands had big knuckles from what appeared to be frequent fighting—perhaps he fought for money in taverns. His long unkempt beard was full of dirt. He did not have the look of a spy, but more like the stableman who cared for a spy's horse. He slumped.

"Do you have a loved one? Wife? Girl friend?"

"Yes," came the answer.

"Do you want to see her again?"

"Yes."

"Think about her. I will be back in a minute."

As he rode toward spy number two he heard the Long Bow escort one say, "You did well. He seemed pleased with your answer."

Spy two was very young. His patchy dark beard had not been shaved in perhaps two weeks—he scratched his chin on the coarse rope. Strong hands matched his lean but muscular body. He sat with a straight back and head held high.

Spy three was very thin, and had been a prisoner of war as indicated by the branding scar on his forearm. His sideburns, nose, and ear hair was wiry and dark, contrasting with his sunburned leathery skin.

Oscar repeated the same procedure with the other spies.

He returned to the short spy.

"What is your motivation for joining the Saraton militia?"

"I was promised gold after the invasion was successful."

"What are your duties for this gold?"

There was a long pause. Although Oscar could not see short one's eyes, the slight movements of his head helped Oscar imagine that the spy was searching for an answer.

"To fight the evil empire of Manshire."

"And what would you do with the gold?"

"Pay off debtors."

Oscar nodded to the Long Bow trio. A Long Bow clapped his hands, another said, "Ouch!"

Oscar noticed the spies reacting to the sound. "Lying only escalates the pain."

The same questions were presented to the young spy. He answered the "what duties" question with "To be a willing spy." And his answer to the use of the gold was, "Start a family."

Oscar followed the line of questioning with the thin prisoner, who answered the "what duties" question with "To destroy Manshire."

He waited, and then nodded at the Long Bow trio. Like before, the spies reacted to the yelp.

Oscar nodded to the Long Bow trio and held up two fingers. A saddle on the ground was whipped with a couple of willow limbs. After the third whip, a member of the trio screamed.

Riding his horse to the young spy, Oscar leaned over and whispered, "Is she a wife or a girlfriend?"

"Girlfriend."

"Is she pretty?"

"She is."

"How does she make you feel?"

"Warm inside. And she makes me want to be a good father and husband."

"Have you been thinking about her this morning?"

"Very much, sir."

Oscar smiled. He had found a young man with integrity and a future with plans. He probably volunteered for this duty thinking the payoff would help him fulfill his dreams. Argo or Cromwell likely thought the money was his only motivation.

"Tell me what I need to know, and you will see your girlfriend again."

"What assurances do I have?"

Oscar liked this farmer. "How big is the militia?"

"The militia has three hundred soldiers."

"Do you know their purpose?" Oscar continued.

"Protect the border between Saraton and Manshire. Also seventy will be assigned to protect Saraton castle."

"When will the militia be in Saraton?"

"They hope to have the border secured in eight more days."

Oscar raised two fingers to the trio. They whipped the saddle and yelped again.

The other two spies repeated the same story. Unfortunately, the information had no tactical value.

Kendrick had told Oscar the militia was closer to seven hundred. In eight days the militia could march through Manshire. He assumed it was all part of a ruse for Manshire to under-defend the border.

Hopefully, with Kendrick's information the puzzle would be completed. "I am going to confine you to this location. It is for your safety. When victory is complete, we will let you return to your home."

Oscar rode to Zachary. "The young spy is to be confined here. Place the others in the barracks jail."

Spies | seipS

Kendrick waited a few minutes before standing—gauging the difficulty from the second effort, he was confident the horse would not cooperate with another take-down.

He looked to the sky after two lone raindrops spotted his sleeve. Another typical spring day; dark clouds gathered, wind gusts developed, and thunder rumbled in the west. Within thirty minutes, rain would be falling. Kendrick had to follow close enough to track hoof prints and far enough to avoid detection. An aggravating suspicion they would not stop for the rain, or the advancing evening would lead to a third night of little to no sleep, further challenged his concentration. He shivered at the thought of again doing a spy's work while wet, and cold.

He felt the perfect calamity blossoming. The tracks would be difficult to detect under the thick cloudy sky, the rain would soon be turning the evidence to mud, and he could not start a warming fire because it would reveal his position.

He rode for another hour until he caught a glimpse of a small campfire surrounded by three men. Stopping to consider his options, he felt an uneasiness possess him.

Every muscle and thought persuaded him to leave. He tugged the reins to the left and travelled over his horse's fresh tracks. About half an hour later he decided sleep was imperative. He could have been easily captured had he missed the dim orange glow of the small fire.

It was better to have some information for Oscar than to be caught and unable to deliver the vital information he did have. Kendrick walked his horse a hundred yards off the road, supported the saddle blanket over a limb and two sticks, and leaned against the trunk to sleep.

Morning arrived. Damp clothes chilled his skin but not his mind.

Back in the saddle, he approached last night's retreat point. Looking at the road, he did not see new tracks. For two plus hours he let the horse walk slowly so he could scan for tracks and the area on either side for clues. His only logical conclusion was the three men had moved during the night's rain—similar to the soldiers from the cave.

A few branches snapped bringing him to the present. He drew an arrow from the quiver. While he searched for the source of the noise, he pulled the bow over his head. Two deer ran across the road. Kendrick did not want an encounter with whatever was chasing the deer. Immediately, he jerked the reins, retreating to a safe location. He dropped behind the crest of a hill, dismounted, and watched the road.

The three men that had raced past him yesterday exited the forest onto the road. One leaned over with his hands on his knees as he breathed heavily. The other two chased the deer into the forest. They must be an advance team finding food for the militia, which was a day away from this location. It would take all day to hunt and prepare food for seven hundred warriors.

The old information combined with the new did not make sense, but he knew it was somehow connected. He rolled onto his back below the hill's crest, waiting for the hunters to clear the area. As the sound of the hunt faded, a distant muffled chatter replaced it.

Silent like a ghost he moved through the forest toward the chatter. Slowing his approach, he stopped at ten to fifteen feet intervals to check the surroundings.

Halfway around the encampment he settled behind a boulder partially covered by a pair of willows. Kendrick rubbed his eyes before staring at the frightening scene—numerous Long Bows sitting together listening to Cromwell. Victor sat next to the knights. Kendrick rolled back behind the boulder. He had to deliver this information to Oscar right away.

Hastily backtracking and carefully stepping to avoid detection, he hoped his horse had not wandered too far. Before leaving the encampment he spied one last time. Cromwell, Victor, and two Long Bows rode horses through the forest heading for the road.

Confusion filled his head. Thoughts of treason by Long Bows, or warriors dressed like Long Bows. What did Reginald say about the kidnappers uniforms? Oh yes, no green collar band.

* * *

Kendrick followed Cromwell, Victor, and escorts late into the night until they stopped at a similar encampment: no campfires, soldiers sleeping on the ground, ten sentries, and a chorus of snoring.

From the top of the cliff Kendrick watched as their morning started early. Warriors woke each other with little talking. Some stretching while others ate food from a cloth bag. He recognized the leader who had talked to the soldiers he had followed to the other encampment. In the one and a half days of following, he had come full circle.

* * *

Althea bathed Oscar's feet with the cool water from the stream, applied Bernard's sweet smelling ointment, and covered them with fresh cloth bandages. Oscar noticed several knights with satisfied smiles watching her. He concluded they were proud to protect a queen that cared enough to treat a wounded subject.

Seeking comfort she asked Oscar, "Are you worried about Kendrick being late?"

"If he does not show today we will send a detail out to find him. He is most likely gathering valuable information," Oscar replied. Or, he has been captured.

For Oscar, quiet days existed before every battle, each side finalizing strategy and tactics, collecting information from spies, and staging the troops for battle. But he was information bankrupt—the slight volume was weak in quality. He had a few

147

contingency plans in his mind. But to have any hope of defending his country, he needed Kendrick to deliver the golden egg.

He had spent six hours lying on the ground with his feet resting on Althea's saddle when Kendrick arrived. Two Long Bows helped Oscar onto his horse. Zachary walked over to join the conversation.

Kendrick was preparing to ask about Oscar's feet, but stopped when Oscar held up his hand and said, "My feet are going to be fine. We might be running out of time. Report your observations so we can formulate our defenses."

His son dismounted before he provided the detail of the one hundred Long Bows, the green collar bars, the location of the militia, the deer hunters, and the locations of the two companies.

"Did you recognize any of the Long Bows?" asked Oscar.

"No, but I only had glimpses of a few warriors," Kendrick replied.

"Were their uniforms, exactly the same, or did they have a handful of slight differences?"

Kendrick looked to the ground and rubbed both hands on top of his head. "The uniforms looked the same. Thinking about it now, they reminded me of children's new Easter clothes—fresh, no stains from eating or working, and stiff unwashed material."

Althea had walked up behind Kendrick. "I think that means they are planning on infiltrating the castle disguised as Long Bows. They do not need disguises to overtake the farming region, or Manshire Harbor." She kissed Kendrick on the cheek. "Nice to have you back."

"The green bars—did Reginald say they were missing, but you saw the bars on the collars?" Oscar asked.

"Yes. It appears they learned quickly from that mistake," Kendrick said.

"We need to distinguish which Long Bows are counterfeit warriors or real knights."

"Remove the green bar from the real knights' clothing," Althea offered.

Kendrick looked at Oscar, "Its simple and clever." A single nod confirmed his approval.

For Long Bow leadership protection, Oscar had only two knight classifications—green bars for knights, and no green bars for leaders—valuable enemy soldiers could be identified by an increasing number of ribbons, buttons, or bars.

"Zachary, order the green bars removed from all Long Bows," Oscar said.

Oscar closed his eyes and rested his chin in both palms. His eyebrows lifted twice, and his head tilted once. He opened his eyes. "These counterfeit long bows, on foot or horseback?"

"About half and half."

Unable to pace, he was surprised how restraining a saddle could be. "Kendrick, draw a map."

Kendrick began by picking and rearranging the debris on the ground. "These three short sticks represent the Manshire harbor, that rock pile is Manshire castle, and the pine cones are the farming region. There are two companies of warriors." Kendrick placed two apple sized black rocks on the map. "They are traveling about six hours at night and hiding during the day. I am guessing they are waiting on the militia to catch up.

"Where is Cromwell?" Oscar asked.

"He is with this warrior company over here." Kendrick pointed to the black rock in the east.

"Hmm. Where is the militia? And the deer hunters?"

Kendrick spread a handful of pine needles in the far south. "That many soldiers will be slow moving. The deer hunters are gathering and preparing food a day ahead of the Saraton Militia." He pointed to the pine needles before placing three small stones near the militia. "We can monitor the location of the hunters and know the militia's position."

Oscar's eyes darted from the militia, the locations of the warrior companies, and the potential targets. With his hands, he blocked map portions to focus his mind.

"Kendrick. Althea. Come here to look at the map." They stood beside his horse. "Notice the gap between the western and the eastern company. I think that is where Cromwell expects the Long Bows to travel and defend against the seven hundred militia."

Zachary joined in the hand shielding.

"The companies could have two purposes—to capture our Long Bows, and to attack a target. If I wanted to control the harbor, castle, and farming region—my primary objective would be the castle. And, the best way to casually overthrow a reigning government would be slipping disguised warriors into the castle's key locations. Like the twins kidnapping, Argo expects us to race into an obvious battle with the militia. Argo wanted us to see the warriors being transported to Saraton." Oscar closed his eyes and placed his hands on the back of his head. A few minutes later Oscar said, "My queen, I am suggesting a risky offensive strategy that will need your approval."

"Tell me your plan."

* * *

It was a clear morning with a few wispy, almost transparent, orange clouds painted by the sun's pre-dawn announcement. On these two mornings, from the observation post used for the twins kidnapping, Cromwell enjoyed the cool crisp silence. He pressed his lips and slightly shook his head when the bell rang. Quentin walked across the drawbridge five minutes later. The king talked to the sergeant, paced occasionally, and twitched with the double bell. The sergeant and Quentin shook hands. After he mounted his horse, the sergeant signaled the army to march.

Two days prior, Cromwell had been surprised and concerned when the spy had informed him of the Manshire Army. Yesterday, he assigned Curtis to lead the militia. Today, he considered it a blessing. When the able bodied men began their march to engage the much larger Saraton Militia he realized they would not be available to aid the Long Bows

In four hours, with little military resistance, he would ride into the castle with one hundred disguised Long Bows declaring victory. By the time anyone discovered the maneuver, he would have seized the castle. In five days, the new army and Long Bows would be captured, pinched between the militia and the balance of the companies.

* * *

Oscar was awake at dawn. He signaled to Kendrick, pacing near the sleeping Althea.

"Good morning. Are you ready for another day in the saddle?" Kendrick asked.

"Yes. Do you feel it? Everything is at the ready—today is the day!"

"Might explain why I am so restless this morning."

Kendrick carried Oscar to his horse.

"This is nature's way of keeping a balance. Now it is my turn to be embarrassed as my son hauls me to my horse. Similar to your feelings when you respond 'Yes, Oscar sir'."

A grin dimpled Kendrick's cheeks. "Yes, Oscar sir."

It took a few moments to adjust his feet, minimizing the pain; he then rode twenty feet to the map, which was updated with each spy report.

"In an hour the five Long Bow squads will begin their surprise hit-and-run attacks on the militia. The army is unpredictable marching toward the militia, which we hope makes us appear as a larger military force, and influences the Saraton Militia to change their plans based on our movements," Oscar whispered as he stroked his chin.

The Long Bows are spread too thin. The newly organized Manshire Army is not combat tested. This battle will be the largest in Manshire history. I am compromised by the lack of field observations from trained spies.

The crisp morning breeze did little to cool his sweating torso.

"If Cromwell attacks the castle, it will be the perfect day," Kendrick said.

"Yes. If..."

* * *

Midday from the bell tower, Kendrick watched Cromwell, in full Long Bow uniform with green bars, lead the one hundred counterfeit Long Bows to the moat, wait for the draw bridge, then routinely enter inside the castle walls. Cromwell's dignified and commanding posture might have been enough to lower the bridge, regardless of Kendrick's instructions.

Along with Oscar, Kendrick worried that either a warrior or knight would start hurling arrows igniting a real battle. And develop it would—over the slightest of insults. He, neither Oscar, nor Althea had anticipated the power of the green collar bars, or lack of them.

A thirsty green barred "Long Bow" warrior arriving at a well, took the ladle from a bar-less knight. Tensions were high as the brawl over who drank first blossomed from a shoving match into a six-knight/warrior skirmish escalating to a castle wide confrontation within minutes.

Kendrick watched as pride and battlefield confusion spread quickly amongst the two forces. The noise was horrific—yells, clanks, arrows, charges, pain, and death.

He was thankful the fifty authentic Long Bows had been ordered to surrender after offering a reasonable resistance; otherwise Manshire would have lost a significant portion of the Long Bow knights.

Kendrick watched Cromwell run across the courtyard into the castle. Twenty minutes later he escorted Quentin to the Manshire Cathedral. Guards were posted at the three exits. Cromwell exited the wagon gate where he blended in with the soldiers setting up in the marketplace.

Waiting a few minutes before leaving the bell tower. Kendrick walked slowly down the twenty-one stone steps, carrying his boots and sword to prevent discovery. At the bottom, he peered around the corner and made eye contact with Quentin, who scanned the cathedral doors before waving him in. Kendrick stepped off the last two stairs and continued to check for warriors.

Placing an index finger over his lips, he said. "We need to whisper to avoid detection."

"Why are you in the cathedral?"

"I have been removed as king and confined here. I think to protect me from Victor."

Kendrick made eye contact with Quentin occasionally while watching for shadows through the stained glass windows. "Did you hear any information regarding troop losses before surrendering your job?"

"Cromwell thinks he lost about twenty warriors, most of which are wounded. We have twelve wounded knights and four dead. It might have been worse had we not planned a surrender," Quentin replied.

"Any idea where he went a few minutes ago? I lost him in the crowd." Kendrick pointed in the direction of the market.

"They are separating the knight Long Bows from the warrior Long Bows. The knight Long Bows will be held in the Assembly Hall and the barrack's jail through the night."

"The Assembly Hall?" Kendrick's face went white. "Is our cache untouched?"

"Yes. It is unbelievable. It was an insightful suggestion by Queen Althea."

A shadow moved across the stained glass windows on the long wall. Kendrick hid between the benches.

"Kendrick, it's okay. A shadow just went the other way." Quentin waited for Kendrick to stand. "You need to know that Victor was permitted to complete Argo's orders to assassinate you, Althea, and Oscar. Cromwell told Victor that I was off the list until the battle was over."

Kendrick rubbed his chin. He stared at the altar a few moments. "Anything else?"

"Five minutes before the escort to the cathedral, two warriors were pushed into the Assembly Hall by Cromwell. One checked for scars on his shoulder, apparently Cromwell whipped him with an arrow. 'Why are you so angry?' The other added, 'I did not know it was the queen's chambers. Some great loot, why would you care?'"

"Thanks, Quentin. I must deliver this information to Oscar. Until you hear differently, we stick with the plan."

"One last thing, he might be changing the purpose of the militia by assigning 'Curtis'. Strangely, Cromwell did not seem to care what I heard." Quentin mocked a salute, but his voice was quite serious. "Until tomorrow."

Kendrick started to leave. The doors are guarded. Maybe I can repel down the outside wall behind the altar. Perhaps Quentin can create a distraction while I slip out the door. His farrowed brow conveyed a deep trouble.

"You look concerned. Can I help?" Quentin asked.

"I am trapped. All the exits are guarded."

* * *

In former Saraton, the rolling hills had been quartered into fields planted with a variety of wheat, oats, barley, legumes, or cotton. The lush green plants were one to four inches high. A line of closely planted trees stood tall against the wind on most of the quarters' west side. A three to six foot hedge of flowering bushes decorated the other field property lines. The combination of roads lined a distorted chessboard.

"Although most of the militia are pawns, their movements have the rhythm of a chess match. The narrow roads through the Saraton farming region are slowing the militia. A small group clogs the roads for fifteen minutes; the roads are emptied only to become blocked again." Zachary said. "Dust plumes reveal the position of Argo's militia. The rear warriors are watching the ground to keep the dirt from their eyes, which makes them easy hit-and-run targets for the five companies of Long Bow knights. Other strategies focus on narrow valleys where two companies catch the militia in a temporary cross fire."

"Are we slowing the militia?" Oscar asked.

"The clogged roads and two days of limited engagements have slowed the militia by a day and a half," Zachary informed Oscar. "Also, on my trip I watched the Manshire Army divide to practice a flanking maneuver, then regroup."

"If these tactics do not delay the militia by three days, we will be in severe trouble."

* * *

Quentin searched the nave, "I have a solution, follow me."

He walked behind the altar, opened the curtain, and pushed the stone panel of Jesus on the cross. It swung open revealing a ladder descending to a passageway.

"Go to the right, it ends in a large secluded room. Go to the left to exit in the boulder field outside the castle. Pull the knot at the bottom to close the panel. Wait for a moment." Quentin abruptly disappeared, and quickly returned. "Light a torch with this candle. God's speed."

"You are on Victor's list and Cromwell could change his mind, you should consider hiding in here for a day."

Kendrick lit the torch, pulled the knot, turned left. He crouched in the shallow tunnel holding the torch ahead of his position and reviewed the day's events. Oscar's best plan was almost destroyed by an ego triggering an uncontrollable avalanche of arrows. And, tomorrow was more dependent on several key elements.

He walked through the passageway until encountering a ladder. At the top rung, he inspected the stone slab. He did not find a knot to pull and attempted to lift it. Holding the torch close to the edges he found a strip of lighter colored stone. He pushed the end of the square slab—it shifted the width of a rose's stem. Repositioning on the ladder, Kendrick had a better angle to push. He stiffened his arms and the slab opened in the middle of four large boulders. Placing the torch in one of the open rings, he climbed the ladder, pushed the square stone back into place, and scattered the vegetation around and over the slab.

Pausing to evaluate his surroundings, he saw a large shadow briskly walk next to the outer wall. The dark figure ran from the corner of the wall, a few seconds later a horse galloped by his position. His jaw dropped and his eyes opened wide when he saw the single white eye, reminding him of the moon.

* * *

"Rumors have been awful. Are they true?" Althea's long face imparted her concern.

Oscar, who had joined the conversation on his horse, leaned forward.

"A fight broke out at a well over a green bar Long Bow that had not conceded position to a bar-less Long Bow, the warriors not knowing the honor code, and the knights knowing any green bar belonged to the enemy." Kendrick's arm gestures widened as the scale of the fighting increased. "Other knights and warriors joined in. The fighting continued to escalate. We held our ground against the counterfeit Long Bows." His arms quickly spread. "Most of our knights fought for a while, then surrendering as planned."

"How many knights did we lose?" Althea asked.

"Four dead and twelve wounded. They are being held with other captives in the Assembly Hall and allowed medical attention."

"How many enemy warriors?" Oscar asked.

"Twenty—all wounded as we planned. Remind me again why we only wounded the warriors."

"They are fighting based on a lie, expecting to be paid in gold that Argo said we took from Saraton. I think the warriors will lose their motivation when the truth is revealed. Killing should be our last resort with innocent warriors," Oscar replied.

"Speaking of innocent, how is Quentin?" Althea asked.

"He was in the Assembly Hall, but was later confined to the cathedral. I think to keep him from organizing his escape using the Long Bows," Kendrick replied. "And a sign that he is no longer the king."

"Did they not guard the cathedral exits?" Oscar asked.

"Yes, two at each door."

"How did you escape?"

"Did you know there is a tunnel system under the cathedral?" Kendrick replied.

"No."

"It is there and in good condition. Access is through the altar's back."

"Cromwell?"

"He ordered Victor to assassinate Althea, you, and me. Quentin is being spared for now. I watched him slink along the outer wall, get on a horse, and ride by my position."

Enemy or Friend

He was dressed as a common man in a dull grey tunic and a monk's hat, carrying a sack with food, extra shirts, and a knife. He was able to move about with ease at the Cyphera port. Alone, for the first time since birth, made him uncomfortable, still he knew how to use a knife.

Victor's assertion had planted a seed of doubt. And Oscar had been extricated from Venela. Would his elaborate scheme unravel? Perhaps a bit of mending was what the plan needed.

He boarded the ship, paid the fat, dirty captain with eight small gold coins. Argo thought the captain would be a good beggar—he tested each coin with his teeth and smelled of grog.

At sea, Argo walked the deck and observed the lazy sailors. He could make this crew ship-shape with a few decapitated hands. Apparently, the captain consumed his weight in grog as the ship was in desperate condition.

When he was young, sleeping on the carriage floor during long trips had made the time go by faster. He searched the deck for a place to sleep—he needed this ship to arrive at Manshire Harbor as quickly as possible.

Awakened suddenly when the gliding ship struck the fixed dock, he stood and stretched. The dock area led him to the shoreline where Cromwell, and the driver of a faded yellow carriage, waited for him.

Cromwell paced angrily. Argo's arrival had evidently removed him from his task and revealed his dedication to succeed. Argo smiled. He waved to Cromwell from the top of the gangplank.

Cromwell pointed at the driver. "Well, help him to the carriage!" He yelled before the driver ran along the dock system to escort him.

"The ship was four hours late leaving Port Welton." Argo pointed at the iron bracket at the carriage's rear. "Tie your horse there and ride with me." He noticed Cromwell's ears were turning red. "We have a lot to talk about." Following Argo into the carriage, Cromwell rolled his eyes.

Cromwell sat with his back against the inside corner. His arms and legs crossed.

After five minutes of silence, Argo asked, "Have we captured the castle?"

"Yes, King Argo. But our control is delicate at best. A few days of submission will subdue your new subjects."

"Has Victor completed his assignments?"

"No. I had him travel with me because he has good fighting skills."

Argo knew that was not a lie, as Cromwell dropped eye contact, but he was sure it was not the full truth.

"He started out yesterday." Cromwell added.

"Why the delay?"

"I was not certain of his loyalty until yesterday's attack."

That seems reasonable. "Tomorrow, I want to evacuate the village and castle so we can turn them to ash and rubble."

Cromwell moved across from Argo. He leaned forward, his hands resting on the edge of the padded bench. Staring down on Argo, he said, "I must insist we wait for the militia. We will need overwhelming strength to peacefully compel an evacuation. What do you expect the citizens to do?"

"Who cares? They have all summer to construct new huts." Argo stared into Cromwell's eyes. "Are you refusing to execute my orders?"

"No! But I am challenging the timing."

"Then you have five days to start the evacuation."

"While you are open to my suggestions." A sly smile wrinkled the corners of his mouth. "Please consider staying at the king's hunting lodge for a few days, or until the castle is secure."

"I will visit Manshire tomorrow."

"My king, might I ask why you are pressing the battle plans?"

"I want you to take charge of rebuilding Saraton Castle. I need a place to rule the new nation of Argotan."

Cromwell opened the carriage door, gripped the window frame, and leaned out of the moving carriage. "Driver, take us to the hunting lodge."

* * *

For Cromwell, the unraveling began the night before with two guards announcing Argo's surprise arrival. Then this morning the ship was four hours late, the side trip to the lodge was six hours, gathering firewood and supper had taken another two hours, then he had to grill the rabbit. He was happy the lodge had no wine, but waited for Argo to sleep. The driver would stay until Argo woke.

He had been absent for too long, and rode through the night. At dawn he was still fifteen miles from Manshire Castle and worried about any consequences resulting from his absence. At one mile, the large cathedral bell rang four times.

At a quarter mile he heard men yelling. A hundred yards from the forest's edge he dismounted as the horse slowed. He could not believe his eyes. Guessing only seventy Long Bows charged the castle, he wondered how the under-manned assault might gain access to the castle with the drawbridge under his command.

The knights on foot stopped occasionally shooting arrows. Cromwell was surprised by the knights' accuracy as several warriors fell or disappeared from the battlements.

The Manshire flag had been rehung. He could see arrows flying from inside toward the warriors on the wall. Twenty knights on horseback waited across the moat for the lowering drawbridge. This, among other things, incensed him.

How did they get knights inside the castle walls without being noticed? The patrols were heavy last night. Perhaps they were hiding before my attack. How could Manshire know?

* * *

A light morning breeze had gently urged the rising smoke to the north. The smell of the burning woods reminded Kendrick of Mother's breakfast eggs. He missed her and the simpler life of an adolescent.

The Long Bow knights had deployed an hour before dawn and waited for the signal from the bell tower. Kendrick waited for the long shadows to slip down the castle walls. For the attacking knights the targets would be well lit. For the defending warriors the dark clothed knights would be difficult to discern.

The shadows receded halfway down the castle walls. The knights would have about half an hour to take advantage of the shadows. Kendrick looked to the cathedral bell tower. Quentin waved when Kendrick signaled with the yellow flag. A minute later the bell rang four times, filling the silence with knights yelling and running toward the castle.

The knights held in the Assembly Room, and those hiding in village houses, began their tasks of securing the drawbridge, and trapping the warriors between two knight forces.

* * *

Kendrick watched as the drawbridge stopped a colt's height above the ground. Four knights dismounted, crawled onto the bridge—their jumping did not dislodge it, while two knights waiving their arms, cleared a path through the waiting Long Bows. At twenty yards from the bridge they turned their horses and ran full gallop, with three yards to go jumped onto the tongue of the bridge, which instantly dropped. The remaining mounted knights galloped over the bridge followed by thirty Long Bows on foot that had hid in the surrounding forest.

Sitting in the saddle waiting for Quentin to ring the bell once, Kendrick was startled when he saw Cromwell, the head of the snake. On one knee toying with a few stones in his left hand, Cromwell tossed the stones into the dirt.

Kendrick casually removed an arrow from the quiver, placed it in the bow, and drew the string past his cheek.

Cromwell stood. The arrow flew past him before it struck a tree.

Cromwell flinched and glared in the direction of the arrow's flight before making eye contact with Kendrick riding full speed toward him. Cromwell ran toward his horse.

Before chasing Cromwell into the forest, the bell rang. Kendrick checked the battlefield. In the distance a rider was racing toward him. It was Victor.

He steered his horse to chase Cromwell. Kendrick was not going to let this man get away this time.

Kendrick slowed to a trot avoiding tree limbs.

Cromwell had just reached his horse. Kendrick, within a spear's length, leaped to tackle him. They rolled twice. Kendrick stood with the speed of a falcon and a split instant slower than Cromwell. He dodged Cromwell's sword tip thrust at his heart, drawing his sword in time to deflect the second lunge.

After a minute's exchange of sword skills, beads of sweat had formed on Cromwell's forehead. Kendrick knew he could not match the combination of Cromwell's skill and strength, but he had speed, his edge to defeat this brute.

Cromwell easily blocked his advances.

"In a moment you will have to defend against Victor and myself," Cromwell gloated.

"But only briefly, as three Long Bows are closely hounding Victor."

Cromwell stepped back to look over his shoulder.

Kendrick prepared for a sword assault, when suddenly a sharp pain flared from his right thigh—the same leg injured at the Knight Games. Victor, on horseback, had aimed the arrow through the narrow target created when Cromwell had twisted to locate the three Long Bows.

Kendrick dared not look away from Cromwell. He could see the arrow's fletching, and Victor along the edge of his vision. Cromwell had instantly changed tactics; he swatted the arrow with the side of his sword. Kendrick clinched his jaw with each thwack.

The volley of three arrows striking high in the trees was louder than woodpeckers.

In that instant Kendrick decided the distracted Cromwell was more valuable alive and stabbed his sword hand. An angry growl covered any sound the sword made as it hit the ground.

Kendrick focused on the area behind Cromwell and was preparing to stop Victor with his bow. Suddenly a large fist struck him below the eye. He fell backwards landing on his back. Kendrick shook his head.

Cromwell collected his sword before mounting his horse. "Another time Kendrick!" He said, cradling the bloody right hand in his left elbow.

Why had Cromwell missed the opportunity to kill him?

Before Kendrick could stand and fly an arrow, Victor was descending from his galloping horse, his boots thumping loudly on the dry grass—three large steps stopped his momentum as he simultaneously drew his sword.

"In another world, we would have been true friends, but you executed my father in this world," Victor said.

Kendrick stood slowly, keeping his eyes on Victor, avoiding any contact with the arrow in his thigh, and aiming his sword at his friend's chest.

"Hunter? You are his son?"

"Yes."

"Kendrick. Duck!" The yell came from behind Victor.

Victor turned as Kendrick fell to the ground.

"Surrender or die!" came another yell.

Victor alternated glances between the sitting Kendrick and the pursuing Long Bows. Victor, swift for a tall man, ran toward his horse and catapulted over its rump.

"This is not over." He pointed at Kendrick while leaning over the mane. Two arrows cleared his back.

Kendrick removed the arrow from his thigh, quickly bandaged the wound with a shirtsleeve, and climbed in the saddle. He thanked the Long Bows, directed the horse, and galloped after his former friend. He was five minutes behind Victor and could not control his jumbled thoughts—the enjoyable hunts, fun stories of the market, revenge for Hunter's death, a deceptive friend.

The trail exited the tree line along a willowed stream. Kendrick stopped when he saw the horse, without Victor.

Suddenly, Kendrick was knocked from his horse by Exeter.

An arrow whispered above his saddle—where his heart would have been.

Victor had selected an area of thick willows next to a beaver pond. Kendrick assumed his former friend wished to use the moist grass to quiet his footsteps.

"Kendrick, I have you in my sights," Victor said.

It was enough words for Kendrick to focus his scanning for a target.

There! A black tunic contrasted with the surrounding greenish beige limbs. He released an arrow at the slight movement and heard a yelp. He loaded another arrow.

"Victor. You should surrender. I have a full quiver. From our red deer hunts you know I can find you with every arrow." He was exposed, standing on the trail. Still he knew Victor had to stand to discharge an arrow, which gave Kendrick enough time to evade it.

He heard shuffling against the half grown leaves and shot another arrow.

A muffled groan preceded, "Kendrick, I am coming out." A few seconds later, Victor stood slowly, limping into the open with two arrows in one leg and a bow in his hand. Placing the end to the ground, he leaned on the bow, inhaled, pulled an arrow from his leg as he exhaled—keeping eye contact with Kendrick. He repeated the process for the second arrow.

A strange feeling haunted Kendrick; he could not establish its origin. He lowered his bow. "Wise decision. You can return to your home after a few years in prison."

The metallic flash of the knife released from Victor's hidden hand caught Kendrick by surprise. He arched his back and twisted to his side—the knife slashed through his coat and cut a shallow gash three inches long above his pounding heart.

The two former friends faced each other, Kendrick stooped in the open area, and Victor was head and shoulders above the willow he had walked behind.

Kendrick stood upright. His third arrow was aimed and the string fully stretched.

Victor stared into Kendrick's eyes, slowly drew an arrow from his quiver, and placed it against the string.

"Do you actually want to take a chance with that arrow?" Victor asked.

Kendrick thought of Victor's assignment—killing the people he loved.

Suddenly Victor positioned his bow in a shooting posture.

There was no choice, the third arrow entered Victor's heart.

"I never thought you had it in you to harm me." Victor said with eyes in a wide surprised stare. He began to sway, and then fell to the ground.

Kendrick lowered the bow gradually. Moisture filled the bottom of his eyes.

He wanted to pray. Two hours later, he placed the last stone on the grave.

Kendrick thought of Victor, and how lucky he had been to have Exeter save his life. While walking to his horse he looked at the horseshoe tracks, his footprints, and where he shuffled to stand. Strange there were no paw prints—he quickly checked on both sides of the trail.

* * *

The skirmish with Cromwell, combat with Victor, thigh wound, and chest slash had fatigued Kendrick, but he was needed at the castle—he was Oscar's eyes and one was swelling shut and turning black around the socket.

Running his horse along the trail was further, but faster than cutting through the forest. Rounding the last curve, he heard cheers coming from inside the castle walls. In the open field, a column of dark grey smoke rose from burning the warriors' bows and arrows. Crossing the drawbridge he saw true Long Bow knights escorting the disguised warriors to prison. Six knights guarded a group of warriors outside the castle's main entrance. The operators dumped moat water on the drawbridge as four warriors, guarded by three knights, scrubbed the blood from the bridge.

As he road through the streets, citizens waved and thanked him for saving Manshire.

He tied his horse at the post then rested against it for a few moments before several men patted him on the back and congratulated him for a successful battle.

Limping through the hallway caught the attention of the two Long Bows guarding the door to the Assembly Hall. They whispered thanks as Kendrick entered.

Zachary and six Long Bows were laughing when Kendrick entered the room. "I always wanted to know how it felt to be King. Nice chair. How do I get one?" He said in jest.

Quentin stood by himself. He covered his smile and closed his eyes, and shook his head slightly.

Zachary stood abruptly and lost his balance for a moment when he saw Kendrick. "Excuse me, we were having a little fun." The other men in the room looked like they had swallowed wormy apples.

"Uh, tell me what happened," Kendrick asked in an uncertain voice. He sat and began to redress his thigh wound with the supplies left from caring for the knights yesterday.

"Their leader deserted them. Without a leader, the warriors had no will to fight," Zachary replied. "Two warriors held in the barracks' jail said Cromwell was furious when Cromwell ordered a sentry to prepare his horse, then hid it at the back of the outer wall."

Or he simply did not want to be seen leaving on the heels of a fresh and precarious victory, Kendrick thought. It was strange that Cromwell did not insert himself into the battle but ran when chased.

"What was the message?" Kendrick asked.

"Meet me early morning at Manshire Harbor," Zachary replied.

Could Cromwell be traveling to the harbor to escort Argo or his emissary? Only Argo had the power to make him leave the Manshire castle or shirk his responsibility. I should find Cromwell.

"Send four knights to the grand curve to inform Oscar we have possession of Manshire Castle," Kendrick said.

"We sent two knights about half an hour ago," Quentin replied. "Is it true Oscar lost his feet?"

"No. His feet are healing from torture by Argo," Kendrick covered a small amused smile. The truth got distorted so easily.

"I have ordered a house-to-house search for warriors. We have eighty three in custody," Quentin said.

"Excellent. That implies ten to twenty warriors are unaccounted for, one hundred was an estimate."

"I should see how the cleanups and post-battle activities are going," Zachary said as he exited.

Quentin and Kendrick joined him.

The hay fire was the biggest concern and it appeared to be under control. Broken furniture pieces were being gathered, enemy weapons collected, the drawbridge was almost repaired, and a thorough house-to-house search would take two days to complete.

Returning to the castle's main entrance, the three found Oscar's horse and others tied to the post. A big smile graced Quentin's face. Walking down the hall toward the Assembly Hall the conversation was lively, but something gnawed at Kendrick's stomach.

Oscar and Althea waited in the Assembly Hall. Kendrick informed Oscar of the post battle activities, his encounter with Victor, and the vanishing Cromwell.

"Next time you are faced with a superior swordsman, step closer, reduce the fight zone," Oscar said. He leaned forward, pointed at Kendrick's leg, and whispered, "Is that the same thigh as the Knight Games?"

"Yes." Before Father asked, he replied, "It is not infected."

Oscar sat in one chair and rested his feet on another. Often he placed his hands on the chair seat to push himself up.

"Gather around. We must not forget we have a major issue left to confront—the Saraton Militia. Our solution must consider the castle needs more protection, and the ministers need to be returned to the castle. Our resources are limited—fewer Long

167

Bows for battle and a newly trained army. We need some clever solutions and tactics. Any ideas?" Oscar asked.

Kendrick and Oscar watched Althea leave the room. Oscar followed her with his index finger. Kendrick's shoulder shrug did not answer his father's unasked question.

"Can we starve them by capturing the hunters?" Quentin asked.

"I would expect them to hunt for themselves," Kendrick replied while watching Althea pace in the hall.

"How about sending five more squads hastening the shrinking militia?" Zachary asked.

"That is an option we know. But, I want to keep the available Long Bows at the castle until this conflict is settled," Oscar replied.

Althea entered the room. "Gentlemen, do not stand. Please be patient with me, for this may seem to you like a crazy idea. Could we send ten knights dressed as counterfeit Long Bows, split up the militia into smaller groups, then lead them into capture by our army?"

Kendrick gave an approving nod to Althea.

"I like this idea. We use their disguise against them; claim to be sent by Cromwell with orders to break up the large group to defend against the smaller raids, and maneuver through the defenses," Oscar said.

"How about splitting the army in two so we can complete the capture faster?" Quentin asked.

"I suggest we destroy their weapons and release them after a few days. Our jail is overflowing," Zachary said. "They cannot fight without weapons. Without a leader what is their individual motivation?"

"No leader, no weapons, and hungry. This might work," Oscar added. "Zachary, send five Long Bows to Manshire Harbor and five to Port Welton. They are looking for a large man with one white eye accompanied by an arrogant small man."

* * *

Late that evening, eleven counterfeit Long Bows exchanged clothing with Zachary and ten Long Bow knights.

After an hour of instruction, which included Althea's description of Cromwell and Curtis's friendship, the knights returned to the barracks. Oscar and Kendrick escorted them for safety. There was no time to train replacements should they happen upon nervous uninformed knights.

At dawn, it was a crisp late-spring morning, the bright half moon setting in the west.

The ten Long Bows lead by Zachary rode fast across the repaired drawbridge. Oscar hoped Zachary was correct—they would spend the night with the army.

* * *

Kendrick felt Father was protecting him because of the injuries received from the Cromwell and Victor encounters—and something Oscar would not talk about. His thigh ached, the chest flesh wound stung, and the black eye throbbed with every heartbeat. But, he could fight through the pain.

He paced in the rose garden. Limping slightly while staring at the ground.

Cromwell was the king's man, despite his reaction to Argo's arrival. With Victor's death Cromwell would carryout the assassinations of Oscar, Althea, Quentin, and Kendrick.

The combination of Cromwell's skills and experience paired with Argo's tactical ingenuity was deadly. Both could, in their minds, easily justify revenge. Our experience with Argo validates his ability to devise a scheme that would utilize Cromwell's skills and leave less evidence than a ghost.

Kendrick could not let them escape Manshire. He did not want to be looking over his shoulder. He hobbled to his horse and rode away from the castle.

* * *

Zachary dressed in his regular Long Bow uniform traveled the last mile alone. The army was two hundred yards ahead when he dismounted and walked toward the camp. He approached a sentry to announce his arrival. After a second, the sentry's eyes widened.

"Follow your orders," Zachary said.

The sentry took Zachary's weapons and escorted him with two guards to the sergeant.

Soldiers ate and slept around scattered campfires. Impressed with the distribution of the army in the forest, a surprise attack would be difficult. He heard laughing and story telling as he followed the escort.

The sergeant and Zachary hugged—the eldest members of the Long Bows under Captain Oscar's command.

"Please tell Oscar that we will engage the militia in two days," the sergeant said. "I thought we were going to be a diversion."

"I bring you a new strategy from Oscar. It is risky," Zachary replied.

"Combat is always risky. Tell me about this new strategy," the sergeant said.

"The plan is to split the army into two groups and retreat to separate locations where we can ambush small companies of warriors."

"How do you propose to break the militia into small companies?"

"That is the risky part, for me anyway. I am going as Cromwell's emissary to convince their leader that the new plan offers strategic advantages to end the battle quickly."

"I am happy that it is you, and not me." The sergeant offered a wry smile and nod to Zachary. "Any suggestions for ambush sites between here and the castle?"

"What is your opinion of Dragon's Tail?" asked Zachary. "The ambush can take place at the meadow a half mile before the Tail where the prisoners can be held.

"That is a good choice." The sergeant stroked his chin with his palm as he concentrated on the ground. "I think Devil Heart would be another good choice. It is closer, but the pit might be small for holding three hundred fifty warriors."

"We can deal with that at the end of the day, if we need to."

* * *

At sunrise, Zachary plus ten escorts travelled with half the army to Dragon's Tail where they made preparations for five ambushes. The warriors would be held in the circular formation known as the Dragon's Tail—a large area surrounded on one side by the Dragon's Back treacherous rock formation and the other side by the remains of the volcano that belched up Dragon's Back.

Satisfied with the preparations, Zachary and ten Long Bows rode half an hour to Devil Heart. Black and dark grey stones along the heart-shaped pit defined the twenty-foot walls.

The sergeant greeted Zachary. "We are ready."

"Expect your first prisoners in two hours."

Zachary changed into a counterfeit Long Bow uniform. Then, he and the ten Long Bows left for the militia.

* * *

Zachary realized the five hit-and-run squads continued to work the militia's rear and sides, something they had not considered in the planning. *Our enemy disguises could become a large problem.*

When the dust created by seven hundred marching warriors was in sight, Zachary plus ten guides approached on galloping horses to create a sense of urgency.

Five horsemen greeted them two hundred yards in front of the militia.

"Where are you going?" asked a horseman.

"We bring an urgent message from Cromwell for Curtis," Zachary replied.

"Their full names please."

"Lieutenant Charles Cromwell did not give us Curtis's family name."

"Wait here." Two horsemen returned to the militia and approached a tall slender man with a long ponytail. After a short conversation, the slender leader rode out to meet Zachary.

"Follow us." The three horsemen turned toward the marching militia tailed by Zachary and ten guides. The leader held up his hand and the militia slowly stopped.

Zachary dismounted. The ten Long Bows formed a line behind him. The slender leader dismounted and walked the last fifteen feet to Zachary.

The slender man clutched Zachary's extended hand.

"You must be Curtis," Zachary said. "Cromwell sends his greetings and he is anxious to share a victory drink with you." Zachary placed his left hand on their clasped hands.

Curtis reluctantly placed his left hand on Zachary's.

"Cromwell wants to hasten a complete victory and has sent us to guide the militia through the enemy's forces," Zachary said. He hoped his thoughts or pounding heart did not betray him. The proximity of the seven hundred armed warriors within a hundred yards of his ten knights made him nervous.

Curtis continued to grip Zachary's hand.

"How does he propose to do this?"

"We split the militia into smaller groups for travel speed, and improve the response to the Long Bow squad attacks." Zachary twisted in his saddle and pointed at the Long Bows. "These men have come from the conquered castle and are familiar with Manshire's fighting positions."

"How is one Long Bow going to look with seventy warriors to a hit-and-run team?"

"The team will leave us alone, the warriors will appear as part of the crazy maneuvering."

"This plan does not sound like Cromwell. He rarely changes horses in the middle of the stream. And how can you be sure where their army will be? Our spies have found them to be wandering aimlessly."

Had not prepared for that. Need a reasonable response, quickly. "Correct. But, I was in the room when an uncomfortable

Argo commanded these changes—I think more warriors would comfort him."

"Sounds like Argo." Curtis paced for a minute. "Tell me the plan?"

Zachary pointed to the knights in formation behind him. "We send two of ten companies, led by these disguised Long Bows every two hours through their defenses toward the Manshire Castle. Cromwell has ordered that you coordinate the troop movements, ensuring a quick and successful completion."

Curtis checked the ten knights then twisted to see the militia, he angled his head and raised his eyebrows.

"Should we get started?"

* * *

Within half an hour Curtis had separated the first two warrior groups.

Zachary assigned a Long Bow to each group. He sent one group off and waited five minutes before directing the second group to go.

"We are tired and hungry from the long journey. I am going to gather some food. Where can the guides rest?" Zachary asked— he wanted to contact the hit-and-run teams.

"They can rest anywhere. I will have food brought to them."

The tenor of Curtis's voice told Zachary not to challenge him, at least not yet.

"Thank you."

Zachary and the eight remaining Long Bows ate and rested about fifty yards from the militia. Zachary watched Curtis move amongst the warriors, stopping to talk with small groups.

The last hour felt like a day. Zachary watched Curtis select the next groups.

"The third and fourth warrior groups are ready," Curtis said.

Zachary pointed at two Long Bows. "You know where to go. Guide them to the castle."

"Join me for some food?" Curtis pointed to an area away from the militia with scrub pines sprinkled between downed pines and a small stream.

Zachary wondered why Curtis selected a remote setting, and wondered if he should prepare to defend himself? "I am going to send two warriors out to verify the location of the Manshire Army. They will be back in a couple hours. I will meet you in five minutes." He pointed at the scrub pines.

When Curtis was out of listening range, Zachary sent two Long Bows out to inform the hit-and-run teams of the ambush plans. Looking at the militia on his walk to the scrub pines, Zachary had to control his reaction when he realized how big the militia really was.

"Cromwell and I are friends from boyhood. I would leave this chaos, but I want to support my friend. I hope the gold is worth it," said Curtis while walking to a fallen log.

Curtis was looking for someone to talk to. And, a good choice was someone with no relationship to Cromwell, or Argo.

"I was told not to talk about it." Zachary looked in several directions. "How much did they promise you?"

"More than I could use in a lifetime. I plan on living a long time."

They talked for an hour about family, how they had met Cromwell, their respective homes, and how they had been recruited.

"I need to prepare the fifth and sixth groups."

Zachary was happy the conversation had ended; he had trouble remembering the lies. "I will send the two guides."

Four more groups and two hours to go—Zachary's skin itched from tension.

Forty-five minutes passed when the two Long Bows returned and reported to Zachary, "Everything is okay with the path to the castle."

"Thank you," Zachary said.

Three men came racing toward Curtis after groups five and six had left more than an hour before.

"It is the deer hunters. I forgot about them," Curtis said.

Zachary walked away from Curtis toward the guides. At ten feet away from the guides he said, "Mount up and ride to the camps like your life depends on it, because it does."

"Why are we running?" a knight asked.

"The three cooks might inform Curtis of the captured warriors that are forty five minutes away."

Zachary and the four Long Bows had galloped past the last warrior of the militia.

"Halt!" Curtis yelled.

Zachary glanced over his shoulder; Curtis, the three deer hunters, and the militia's only five horsemen chased Zachary and the four guides.

The time from the militia to Devil Heart was fifty minutes by foot and twenty by horseback. Zachary and guides caught up with the fifth group forty yards from the ambush location. He checked ahead, with no one in sight, the army was prepared for this group.

"The enemy is following!" Zachary shouted at the fifth group. "Prepare for battle!" The warriors turned to face the galloping sound and drew arrows. The forward rows knelt.

He hoped the sergeant waited two minutes before giving the attack command. Capturing the groups was a remarkable accomplishment, but catching a field commander alive was a major coup.

Curtis and his impromptu squad raced toward the partial militia group then stopped at the edge of group.

The confused fifth group warriors looked to each other for guidance. Zachary noticed a lot of shoulder shrugs.

"Stop him, he is a traitor!" Zachary shouted—hoping the sergeant would give the attack order soon.

In that instant, the sergeant gave the charge order and two hundred army soldiers ran from the trees yelling then surrounding Curtis, the impromptu squad, militia group, and Zachary. The army's noisy advance startled the captives. By the time Curtis realized what had happened, it was too late. Not a shot was fired.

Zachary smiled—he knew they were no match for the warriors' skills, but the army's soldiers looked menacing.

"Drop your weapons!" the sergeant barked.

The army, with bows drawn, lined the path to Devil Heart and encircled the warriors. Spaced ten feet apart each warrior was checked for weapons before walking over the rocky terrain down into the large heart shaped cavity.

"You know this is temporary. Cromwell will rescue us," Curtis said.

"Cromwell and Argo are on the run. You have been abandoned." Zachary countered.

* * *

The next day Zachary sought out Curtis from the Devil Heart prisoners. "How was your night?"

"Chilly, but survivable," Curtis said. "We are going to survive? Yes?"

"Oscar is willing to offer your freedom, but there are conditions."

Curtis shrugged his shoulders and tipped his head. "What are the requirements?"

"I want to remind you of our conversation at your arrest. I speak the truth—Cromwell has abandoned you. Before the day fades, many Long Bows will pursue him and Argo for crimes against Manshire," Zachary said.

"I do not understand Cromwell's attachment to Argo. His loyalty is— questionable," Curtis said. A bitter smile appeared as he slowly shook his head. "May we talk about the warriors' release?"

"You travel with the sergeant and me arranging for the remaining militia to surrender. Then you and I will oversee the release of one hundred per day. For each warrior involved in crime, or any military action, you will serve a year in prison."

"That is not acceptable! I cannot be held accountable for the actions of nine hundred warriors."

"The alternative—you will be charged with crimes against Manshire, for which you will serve nine hundred years, or be shot. Your choice. I suggest you practice your best persuasion skills."

* * *

Kendrick had started tracking Cromwell at the site of their shortened fight. He was happy to find Cromwell's horse had a deformed shoe—an iron void where it had rusted out.

Cromwell had stayed on the trail. He must have been in a hurry.

If Argo the king was a late riser, Kendrick could shrink the distance between them, and perhaps catch them by surprise.

Two hours had passed when he stopped two hundred yards from the lodge—no smoke, no horses, and no activity.

Approaching the lodge, he could see Cromwell and another had been housed there a couple days. There were several other horses and one set of carriage tracks, though several days older. The carriage tracks indicated two horses going to the lodge and only one leaving.

Kendrick entered the lodge. The dust on two unmade beds had been wiped off. The dirt on the floor showed signs of fresh footprints. He could feel the heat from a recent fire touching the hearthstones. Outside he located Cromwell's horseshoe tracks—the edges crisp, not rounded by wind or water.

After half an hour he was sure Manshire Harbor was their destination. He kicked the horse's hips. Worse case, they would be two hours ahead. He hoped his experience with ships rarely sailing at the passenger's convenience applied to Cromwell.

The trail crested about half a mile from the harbor. A ship floated away from the dock with a single small sail. Three Long Bows patrolled the dock area.

If Cromwell was arranging his exodus from Manshire, it made sense to keep the horses to the last second. Therefore he was looking for a large man, small man, and two horses.

Kendrick signaled the two Long Bows in the village streets.

"Have you searched the entire village?" he asked.

"No, we have been checking the buildings closest to the docks and progressing outward. We have started over each day in the event they are moving at night."

"I think Cromwell is within the dock and warehouse facilities. He cannot be in public hoping to buy passage, or moving about with hopes that we miss him." Kendrick paused, removed his hat, glanced around, and replaced his hat. "Where are their horses?" he whispered.

Kendrick stepped to the side pointing to the small house on the hill by the harbor channel. "Is that the Harbor Master?"

"Yes sir."

"I will inform him the ships are to be detained until we have checked the three warehouses and four vessels. Search the warehouses in pairs. One Long Bow to stay outside watching the piers and dockworkers, looking for a big man with a white eye. Be careful he is extremely dangerous, and murder does not disturb him."

Kendrick limped to the Harbor Master.

"Good morning. I am..."

"I know who you are. What do you want?" the Harbor Master interrupted.

"Hold all the ships in the harbor until we have searched the warehouses and boats; and, keep any arriving ships in the channel."

"How will I be compensated if I cannot tax the ships?"

Kendrick's sensed his ears turning red. He longed for sleep, but pain kept him awake and shortened his temper. He removed a small leather moneybag from his shirt, grabbed an arrow from his quiver, and stuck the bag to the tabletop.

"Here is your compensation. I will be back for my change when we have completed the search. If a ship exits or enters the harbor before I return, you will be paid, but expect to spend a year in the Manshire prison for each ship." Kendrick leaned on the edge of the table staring down at the master. "Any questions?" Kendrick glared until the Harbor Master diverted his gaze. "I thought not!"

The warehouses had been searched by the time Kendrick returned to the docks. An excited Long Bow blurted out, "We found the horses!"

"Argo and Cromwell must be on a ship," Kendrick said.

In spite of the aching wounds, Kendrick sensed someone watching. He scrutinized the four ships' decks and nothing appeared abnormal.

Kendrick smiled, he could see the harbor master signaling frantically for the ship to return to the dock.

"Where are the horses?"

A Long Bow pointed at the second warehouse, near the first occupied berth.

Kendrick scanned the area before walking up the gangplank.

"Who are you? And, what are you doing on my ship?" said the captain waiting at the top.

"I am the envoy for Queen Althea of Manshire. We are searching this ship for an enemy Lieutenant."

"No one on this ship but crew."

"We are going to search this ship," Kendrick said emphatically.

The captain turned his head and nodded—two men holding swords accompanied the captain.

A moment later two arrows stuck into the back of the rigging gallery. Kendrick checked quickly to find their origin. Both Long Bows, Marcus and Shelton, had reloaded. "What is your order, sir?"

Kendrick turned to the captain. "Your response?"

A soured frown accompanied the captain's words, "Welcome aboard."

"Have your crew gather on the dock," Kendrick commanded.

The ship was empty five minutes later.

Removing his knife from the scabbard as he walked toward the stairs to the darker orlop deck. He was on the fourth step leaning under the deck, when he saw two columns of sunlight pass through the square cargo doors. His heart leaped from his chest, his eyes darting among the shadows. He was much too vulnerable squatting on a staircase with nothing to hide behind, his blackened eye nearly swelled shut.

On the fifth stair he took a deep breath hoping to calm his heart as more of his body became a target. The sixth step was more of the same, except for the increasing stiffness of his thigh.

A quick movement in the shadows between the light columns commanded his focus. Kendrick had turned sideways to reduce his target profile. Before stepping onto the next stair, he paused to listen. A few squeaks and a scurrying noise—rats. A deep breath filled his lungs with the stale smell of stagnate seawater in the bilge.

Suddenly, he lost his balance—step seven was broken. Fighting to right himself, he landed awkwardly on his left ankle when he reached the deck. He clinched his jaw attempting to stand. The pain was worse than the thigh wound.

Limping gingerly, he passed the last light column.

Kendrick was fifteen feet from the end of the deck when he came upon the back of a small man wearing a monk's hat. No, it was impossible.

"Bernard?"

Stored Alone

He felt the rhythm of the ship gliding with the waves. The darkness was wet and pungent. Kendrick's head and left rib cage throbbed with his heartbeat.

"Flaming Dragons!"

"Kendrick?"

The weak voice startled him. "Who is asking?"

"Shelton. Marcus and I boarded the ship with you."

"Where is Marcus?"

"I think he is dead. He is cold and motionless."

"How did he die?"

"Struck on the head with a belay pin, like you. I have the pin over here. It is the only weapon we possess." Kendrick felt inside his left boot.

Even in the dark Kendrick knew the thick, slick, and warm liquid on the back of his head was blood.

"How did you get here?"

"Cromwell tossed me in from the main deck. I think my shoulder is broke."

That may be how I received these broken ribs. "How long ago?"

"Uncertain. You should know that Cromwell has possession of the ship. I was searching near the bow when he slipped the captain aboard for answering some questions. He forced the captain to cooperate, or die. The captain refused—that is when Cromwell threw me into the hold access. I passed out when I hit the bilge."

"Is there a hatch?" Kendrick asked.

"Overhead is my guess. Unless they moved us to a bigger central storage compartment—it could be anywhere." The bilge's curved walls meant they were in the bow under the orlop deck.

Kendrick stood slowly, debating if he should put his weight on the left ankle sprain or the right thigh wound. He stooped to avoid striking his tender head, which placed tension on his excruciating rib cage. Extending both hands along the beam he found a hatch in the ceiling. Stepping directly under the door he was able to lift it six inches.

"Hold that belay pin straight out from your shoulder. I am going to find it by sweeping my hands about," Kendrick said. Several attempts failed before he nudged the pin with his forearm. "Okay, I have it."

Kendrick grimaced and grumbled whenever he shifted too much weight to one leg, or hunched over too far.

Under the hatch he lifted until he could wedge the pin between the cover's side and the floor's flashing. Feeling around the hatch's corners he determined how it was constructed. Repositioning the pin against one of the hatch's weaker joints he pulled on the pin like a lever.

Suddenly, the corner split. He moved the pin to the respective corner and repeated the process. He rested on the bilge controlling his breathing to avoid the broken ribs from puncturing his lung. The few glimmers of light were a refreshing, but temporary reward.

Blood mixed with seawater sloshed with the ship in the bottom of the bilge. Shelton's ashen face had three gashes still leaking blood and four that had started to scab. His broken left shoulder was two inches below the level of his right. Kendrick needed to get Shelton some medical attention or he would die.

He lifted the hatch with his right hand and with his left he felt for what restricted the cover's removal. Kendrick's fingers found simple lacing knots holding the hatch cover. After a few minutes of touching the knots he pulled the end of the rope. The hatch cover lifted off the flashing.

Kendrick sat—his chin resting on his chest. He closed his eyes for a few moments. He heard voices in the hold above. He shook Shelton's good shoulder to wake him, when he did not move Kendrick checked Shelton's breathing.

Shelton was dead.

Kendrick clinched his jaw, suppressed any grumbling, and pulled himself up through the hatchway. He sat by the edge of the hole taking rapid shallow breaths. The voices grew louder—he needed to hide. He placed the cover over the hatch and tied lacing knots, then crawled behind four large coils of inch and a half rope.

* * *

"What do you mean 'he is gone'," Argo asked.

Cromwell watched as he tried to control his reaction. But Argo's flaring nostrils accompanied protruding eyes and a red complexion—conditions Cromwell had witnessed before.

The two sailors glared at each other.

Argo slapped the smaller man. "Well? Your answer?"

"The hatch cover was tied in place, the two knights were dead, and the envoy has disappeared."

Argo rapidly drew Cromwell's sword. Cromwell grabbed Argo's arm. "He cannot help us if he is dead."

Argo slapped the side of the blade against Cromwell's chest. "Here, your sword."

Cromwell had had enough of the imp.

He took his sword, leaned over, and removed Argo's hat. "You almost lost your life," Cromwell said returning his knife to the scabbard. "Argo, you are the king of nowhere. The militia by now has lost its purpose, the Manshire Castle invasion has failed, and we—you and I—are the last two citizens of Saraton. Your arrogance needs to take a long journey, or you will suffer many beatings. I will escort you to the palace, then I am going to sea."

Cromwell could imagine steam coming out his crimson ears. "Our immediate task is to find Kendrick. We need the captain to direct his men."

* * *

He was alone with only a belay pin, and the knife in his left boot—a tactic he had learned from Father. He must battle against the crew, Argo, and Cromwell. Kendrick must assure they never return to Manshire with plans for a future assassination, abduction, or any act of revenge toward his family.

He had only two choices, fight or surrender. The latter was not an option in Kendrick's mind.

Weapons! Where would they store his, Marcus's, and Shelton's weapons? Argo would plan a search starting at the bow and stern attempting to entrap him. He limped to the stern to find places he could hide and prepare for the first attack.

He heard the crew cheering—the search had been unleashed.

Hiding, Kendrick stood with this back to the hull, staring at the top cotton bail.

"Do you think the captain will actually reward the finders?"

"He cannot risk a mutiny. He will pay."

They carried daggers.

Kendrick decided his strategy was to eliminate the search teams and frustrate Cromwell to the point where he entered the search. With the silent movement of a cat, Kendrick struck one of the pair with the pin and stabbed the other with his boot knife. He put their dull daggers between his waist and pants belt.

He limped through the narrow paths created by the random placement of freight and tie downs, pausing before entering the wider path sections.

Whispers gave away their location. Kendrick slipped behind a large wooden crate and waited. He heard a deck board squeak as they passed.

He struck them with the pin, tied their hands, gagged and hid them, then stole their knives.

The hurried movements inflamed his broken ribs. The gash burned like the blacksmith's forge from the salty sweat on his chest. The thigh pain felt eerily similar to his infected thigh after the Knight Games. He closed his eyes, inhaled slowly and exhaled gently. His ribs shot pain throughout his body. He had no choice but to find determination and energy from within.

The oat bin had caught his attention just as the attack began. The ridges resulting from hand smoothing should have settled out during transportation and loading. The crewmember responsible for stowing the three bows, quivers, knives, and swords had simply laid them under a few inches of oats.

Kendrick was convinced some of the crew would have to die to keep him from capture and instill fear in the searchers.

Two more crewmembers entered from the bow hatchway. He struck both in the shoulder with a knife and they exited immediately. Kendrick moved to the middle of the deck, removed his long bow over his head, and prepared an arrow. Two entered from the bow hatch and two from the stern.

The stern shots were more difficult. The arrow struck the first member in the lung and the second man in the stomach. Turning toward the front he loaded and released an arrow that hit a liver. The following arrow found a heart. He adjusted the quiver over his shoulder; the belay pin wedged between his weapons belt and back.

"Are you running out of sailors? You have no choice Cromwell," Kendrick shouted. "I am waiting." He knew he had to battle with Cromwell soon—his body was stiffening from the injuries and he had not eaten since leaving the castle.

Kendrick leaned against a crate. He let his chin rest against his chest until he heard two men enter from the stern hatchway. He was disappointed Cromwell had not accepted the challenge. Kendrick shot arrows and hit both in the right shoulder as they focused on the dead or wounded mates lying at the bottom of the stairs. They returned to the deck above. He wanted the wounded sailors to create fear amongst the crewmembers.

Kendrick heard a sneeze. When he looked to check the bow hatchway, his heart pounded when he saw the large, white-eyed adversary holding a sword in his left hand—Cromwell's weapon of choice was Kendrick's least favorite implement.

Kendrick slowly took a deep breath and after a whimsical head tilt, he shrugged his shoulders and drew his sword while walking calmly toward Cromwell who was surprisingly talkative.

"You were lucky I had to protect my king. Otherwise you would be dead. But that little skirmish told me you are not a swordsman and I am a better with my left hand than you using your preferred hand," Cromwell said. He was twenty-five feet away. "And your father, what a stroke of luck guessing the militia was a ruse. However, you are a knight with honor and I will give you time to pray before you are dispatched."

Kendrick noticed Cromwell waved with his bandaged right hand. Faster than a snake's strike, a sharp pain developed in Kendrick's left hamstring. A crewmember under cover of Cromwell's talkative spree had stepped unnoticed down the stern hatchway.

Kendrick had no time left; he yanked the arrow from his muscle, switched the sword to his left hand, then with his right pulled a knife from his belt. He turned away from Cromwell and struck the archer in the chest.

Immediately he faced Cromwell who had run closer to him, the lieutenant's first jab had been premature, as Kendrick had not fully turned. The sword went through the cotton shirt and nicked his stomach. Withdrawing the sword, Cromwell lifted the blade and cut Kendrick's cheek.

Time slowed for Kendrick as he recalled a comment from his father—move closer against a superior swordsman.

Faster than a blink, Kendrick jabbed twice and attacked moving closer, forcing Cromwell to retreat. Finding the right shoulder before he stepped closer to Cromwell who was unable to quickly draw the sword back enough to deflect the jabs, Kendrick stepped back and stuck him in the left shoulder. He moved closer and struck Cromwell below the Adam's apple with his fist.

Kendrick was fading. He had expended too much energy in the recent combat flurry. He would find success in the next few minutes or collapse on the deck. He stepped back for a momentary rest.

Cromwell also moved back and used his long arms to extend the sword across the extended gap. He thrust at Kendrick who leaned back then followed the withdrawn weapon.

Lieutenant Charles Cromwell sneezed.

Kendrick saw an opportunity. Stepping forward, Kendrick placed the sword under his arm. It was pointed behind his back.

Cromwell tilted his head, lowered his guard, and stopped momentarily to watch the strange swordsmanship.

The lapse was Kendrick's last chance.

Kendrick spun with everything he had left in him, his back inches away from Cromwell's chest, his sword entered Cromwell's heart. He pushed it an extra inch before letting go. Facing Cromwell who was staring down at the silver sword jutting from his torso, he focused temporarily on something behind Kendrick before falling to his knees and collapsing on his face.

Kendrick grabbed Cromwell's sword. He tossed it like a short spear at the location where Cromwell had glanced, just missing a sailor holding a bow.

He limped to the stern stairs. The sailor dropped the bow. Kendrick held eye contact as he removed the sword from the step edge and passed by the sailor.

On deck, the sailors stepped back as he climbed the stairs. He scanned the crowd for Argo.

Kendrick saw a flash of movement in the corner of his eye, dropped to his knee, and deflected the knife with Cromwell's sword.

The sailors backed up a foot.

"Where is Argo?"

Several sailors pointed off port at a boat being rowed by a man with a monk's hat, toward the storm on the horizon.

Amherst Rose

Summer was two weeks away by the calendar. But this morning at Manshire Castle, it felt like mid-spring when the Amherst Rose's fragrance typically occupied the area of the rose garden.

"It is sad that Xage left. I wanted to thank her for delaying the bloom. Strange, she did not say goodbye to anyone," Althea said.

Kendrick scratched the back of his neck. "Yes, strange," he whispered. Same with Bernard and Exeter.

Kendrick followed Althea's tipped head toward Oscar. He was walking on crutches. "Father, thank you for joining us this morning."

"I had forgotten how intoxicating that aroma could be. It brings about pleasant memories of your mother. I have been a fool to miss this day the past two years," Oscar said, the sun reflecting off the tears at the bottom of his eyes.

The shadows retreated from the rose bushes allowing the sunlight to warm and caress the flowering buds.

Althea pointed. "Both of you should be sitting."

A wave of goose bumps trickled down his back as Kendrick took in a deep breath and held it for a few moments.

From the stumps, the line between sun and shadow, light versus dark, blooms versus buds, was evident.

Kendrick thought about the extremes of war—being prepared—hiding Long Bows in the village and the blessing, Argo calling Cromwell away. Being prepared—Althea's escape and the blessing, Bernard and Exeter. Did so much depend on luck or something else?

"I must go, we have ministers to escort, and warriors to send home," Oscar said, standing and hugging his son. Oscar leaned over to Althea, kissed her cheek. He whispered something in her ear.

"What did he whisper?" Kendrick asked when Oscar had left them.

"So you do not know?" she queried, smiling over at him.

Did he? Her smile reminded him that it was appreciating the small acts at big moments that made life possible. A single blooming rose amongst an entire garden. Althea's joy-filled kiss in the thick undergrowth that ended her escape. It was carrying her exhausted body to the clay pot, the kiss when he returned from his spying journey. It was helping her swim to shore. What could possibly bring more joy to his life than those moments?

What did he not know?

Kendrick reached for her hand, and it was then, like the whispering of the waves that Kendrick thought on her 'illness' before the kidnapping, her extreme 'sea sickness' in the stolen boat, her pale face and tired limbs throughout their travels. And a light unlike the sun suddenly penetrated his heart. So, it was true then.

"I was wondering...do you think Oscar will be a good grandfather?"

Preview for

"Summer Swarm"

Coming 2016

Corporal Punishment

Head Master George Ulster's large hand grabbed Luxton's long black hair and lifted him to his tiptoes. He dragged him across the cake and icing, and out the sheet skirted dining room, into the converted confessional area where a lone chair was fixed to the floor. Mid-afternoon meant he could focus on the stained glass dove cast on the west sheet. A hundred plus heads would watch through the wall's seams.

Without a word, Luxton gripped the edge of the seat; Ulster whipped.

Luxton heard the head master's angry whispers, "How can you expect me to protect these children without money?" Whack. "As the rolls increase, the food decreases." Whack. "We are running out of floor space for beds." WHACK.

* * *

Nazar Cathedral, established twenty years ago by the Celestial Glory Church in the remote wilderness of Dashald, had been built for the purpose of taking God to the barbarians. It quickly became the central unifying structure for the rickety village that sprung up along the turbulent river.

Ten years ago, the church had converted rapidly to an orphanage when the river dwindled to a stream during the eighteen-month drought. Many families left children at the cathedral steps, and departed overnight. The head master gave each orphan a name and recorded birthdays as the date they entered the orphanage.

Ropes and sheets crisscrossing the Nave established walls for boys' dormitory, girls' sleeping quarters, nursery, a small dining room, a cramped classroom, narrow hallways, and makeshift washrooms.

On the trio of past annual visits ended with the territorial archbishop had scolded Ulster, for hours over the "deplorable conditions".

* * *

Contributing to the sleepless nights and taking its toll on Ulster's health was pressure from the territorial archbishop, the caring for too many children, the dwindling food and clothing donations, and the vandalizing and pranks by the older misfit boys were a few of the troubles that revealed his tortured soul.

Ulster's skin had a grayish white coloration. His eyes were a permanent red, and his former well fitting clothes hung off his shoulders—he looked like a tall orphan.

The annual clothing donation gathered by the archbishop arrived in the morning. Two boys, one a misfit, and three girls sorted the clothes by size, female, male, and needing repair. The shipment contained worn-out clothes, boldly colored apparel, laced collars, and dirt stains. The variety of dress at dinners and classrooms looked like a mucky spring assortment of wild flowers.

The misfit hid five of the nicest drab shirts in the sorting area for retrieval later, then carried them to Luxton's cot. He looked in every direction before packing them under the cot. Luxton watched the whole episode.

Not wanting another whipping, Luxton waited for the misfit to depart.

He was removing the shirts when the head master walked up from behind. Ulster did not wait.

He grabbed Luxton's legs and dragged him to the modified confessional. "You are too much trouble for this orphanage. You need to change your attitude, mister. Maybe a week of confinement will be a good start."

"But, I did not steal them, I was going to return them to the shipment." Luxton replied. He glanced about grabbing chair and table legs.

"Sure you were."

Arriving at the confessional Luxton stood and fought, his arms and feet flailing, attempting to escape Ulster's grip. He had lost the effort but discovered he would soon have enough strength to defeat Ulster. When the door was locked, Luxton realized there was no place to sit.

Luxton had a week to plan his escape and revenge.

Dark Visions

A violent twitch woke Kendrick. Initially, he could not determine if the impending crash in his nightmare, or the venison pasty was the cause for the fire in his stomach. Althea, slept peacefully. She had had two pasties, which she justified as her favorite food though she ate for two.

Kendrick slid gently from under the covers; his toes found the floor's temperature to be cool, and shivered from the cold air being absorbed into his sweat soaked nightshirt. He sat on the edge of the bed rubbing his eyes before his trek to the kitchen.

Queen Althea groaned. "Are you okay?" she asked. Her silky voice had a blossoming gravelly quality since the start of 'their' pregnancy—she sounded like a drunk awakened outside a tavern.

"My stomach is burning. I am going to the kitchen for some milk," Kendrick replied.

To the kitchen he rubbed his belly and tried to make sense of the nightmare's divergent images.

He finished the half goblet of milk and hunk of bread; the stomach fire was successfully extinguished.

While returning to the queen's chambers, he pondered the vivid nightmare images; the magical appearance of the fifteen ballista siege machines, the bitter odor coming from the drawbridge area, and the tall thin man with cropped white hair was shaking his head while watching from inside the tree line. Kendrick wondered if he knew the man. The strangest image however was one of a large man with long black hair, gathered in a ponytail, riding atop a black Clydesdale laughing as thousands of warriors oozed from the woods attacking the castle.

Counter to the frightening nightmare, a wonderful sensation of flying above the castle, ballistas, and scurrying warriors made him feel invincible.

Upon his return to the queen's chambers he waited outside hoping for the collected intoxicating mix of extreme safety, ultimate power, and blissful freedom to bless his mind, if only briefly.

Quietly he entered the room then closed the door. Tip-toeing in chambers, he prepared to slip silently into bed.

"How are you feeling?" asked Althea. "It is not like you to go to the kitchen."

"Sorry for waking you. I had a strange nightmare—more like a frightening vision which I observed while flying on a large bird," Kendrick replied. "But, the disturbing images are not fully connected."

"Maybe waking will break the nightmare's spell and pleasant dreams will follow."

"I hope your prediction is true."

Kendrick's eyes, though closed, did not aid in his sleep. After an hour of attempting to find a comfortable position, he finally slept.

Kendrick watched his reflection in the stale water, just west of the castle. He was a lad of fourteen. The intoxicating aura had returned and he did not care that he rode a great grey owl the size of a colt. Absorbed in the moment's pleasant mood, unaware of the arrows, he looked to the sky and watched as three black ribbons whisked toward the castle—the smaller ribbon wrapped around his chest. At that instant, he became fully aware of the battle below, that he had no weapons, and was the target for many arrows.

The great owl flew at will—Kendrick could not alter the course—the ground ever closer now. An arrow struck Kendrick in the lung. He cried out in tremendous pain.

Suddenly the owl flapped franticly—a spear found its wing. Kendrick fell.

The owl flew away toward the west. Air rushed by as he fell the full height of the castle wall. His yell was silenced as the air had rushed from his lungs when he slammed into the moat. Submerged, reflex triggered his throat to inhale. Water rushed into the vacant lungs, then his vocal cords swelled like wet leather choking off his throat. Darkness slowly constricted his vision until all was black.

* * *

"Kendrick, relax. Kendrick, wake up!" she shouted. Attempting to hug his flailing arms proved to be unsuccessful. Althea ducked several arm swings, and dodged a couple jabs. Her failed efforts to awaken him gave birth to thoughts that he might be in a trance. She rolled out of the bed, ran to the door, then grabbed the wash water pale.

Whoosh!—the water splashed his face, ran onto the floor, and woke him. She placed the bucket on the floor.

"What happened?...Oh my!...Flaming Dragons!" Kendrick declared. He noticed the floor was wet around her feet. "Are we having a baby?" His chest heaved with every breath.

"No. But that might have been less dramatic than your nightmare," she replied. "Tell me about it."

"It was frightening. I felt possessed and could not wake." His breathing had calmed. "Something held me, forced me to see every image." Kendrick told her about the great grey owl and the pleasure of flying. His smile distorted to a frown when he revealed the black snake like ribbons, painful arrow in his lung, spear in the wing, and helpless feeling of drowning.

* * *

The edges of the two stone steps into the barracks had started to wear. The weathered main door had turned grey from the morning sun. Oscar considered the steps and door functional, along with the interior walls that had water stains from the leaking roof, and the three bunks declared unfit for use. Oscar had diverted the repair money to hiring a Long Bow knight.

Kendrick knocked.

"Come in."

"Good afternoon, Father."

Oscar's private room showed its age as well with four blocks of oak holding up one corner of the cot, and one of the shutters held in place by a singular hinge.

"Good to see you. What brings you to the barracks?" Oscar asked.

"I have come to seek your guidance concerning a nightmare."

"Oh...a nightmare." Oscar focused on Kendrick's eyes expecting to see a hint of teasing. But he saw Kendrick was concerned.

"Not just any nightmare, but a frightening vision like I have never experienced before," Kendrick said. Oscar directed Kendrick to sit on the cot and then moved to the edge of his chair.

"Describe your vision. I might be able to help, though it is a skill I have yet to master." Oscar felt awkward. For a few seconds, he did not know what to do with his hands. His past belief in fate contradicted any potential for reliance on, or prophecy regarding dreams, nightmares, and visions.

"I woke last night after part of the vision revealed the large bird I rode was crashing," Kendrick said while staring at the floor.

"How large?" Oscar asked—not sure where to direct Kendrick. He slid back into the chair and rocked it on the back legs.

"A great grey owl the size of a colt."

Oscar laughed. Then instantly checked Kendrick's eyes. "I am sorry, the thought of a raptor the size of a colt brought a humorous image to mind. Can you visualize those large feet attempting to catch small rodents?" Oscar was happy that Kendrick smiled. "A flying dream—those are delightful...usually. What did you find disturbing?"

"I counted fifteen siege machines aimed at the castle," Kendrick said. "And the air had a bitter smell originating from the drawbridge, but the owl would not fly by. I did see smoke."

197

"Ballistas?"

"Yes."

"Who could afford fifteen—maybe, three? They have to be moved for battle, maintained; and the supplies would be a tremendous burden," Oscar said. "A bitter smell, like old wet oak or tar like?"

"Something I have never smelled before."

"I assume there is more?"

"A tall, thin man with white hair watched from the forest."

Oscar rubbed his beard. "He could be one of a thousand men in Manshire," Oscar, said as much to himself as Kendrick, looked past him. After a few seconds, he stared at Kendrick. "Sorry, you were saying?"

"Three black ribbons raced toward the castle then one separated and wrapped around my chest. My awareness of the danger I faced instantly replaced the euphoria of flying."

Like a flying arrow, Oscar's mind went directly to target—his wife's brother. Oscar set all the chair's legs on the floor. He stood and paced.

"His hair, was it cut short and combed forward?" Oscar asked.

"Yes."

"Did he carry a long white walking stick?"

"Yes."

"Maybe fifty?"

"Yes. Who is he?"

* * *

Richard's rheumatism always flared up before any trip or long walk. At twenty-five the stiff hip and knee joints provided the first hints of a lifetime's pain, and a family's curse as his sister had the same problem but her joint knots grew to the size of plums. Oscar had been understanding and loved Abbey deeply. Richard was thankful for that side of Oscar.

Abbey's brother, now forty-eight, envisioned himself as part mystic, part scholar, and a whole recluse. He struggled with communication—he would wander off if the conversation did not suit his interest—another family curse that he had adjusted to, for it gave him time to study.

He gathered his birch walking stick, the other toga, and a knife for roots and berries. The two-day walk would clear his head and focus his mind on squelching Oscar's reaction. Richard guessed they would continue their fate or free-will debate until the queen interceded. He needed his wits sharper than dragons' teeth to convince the queen, Oscar, and his nephew Kendrick, of their bleak and devastating future.

* * *

Queen Althea was exhausted from the monthly meeting with her subjects—unprepared for the complaints over land ownership and crop retention—two multi-layered complex concepts that would require much discussion and consideration, which she planned to put-off until a few months after the birth— maybe another less intricate matter would replace it.

When the room was empty she stood and stretched. She waddled like a duck to chambers with her hands pushing on her sore back.

Every fiber of her body felt like the weight of large stones rested on her arms, legs, and stomach restricting her movement. Yet a sense of obligation possessed her. She fell asleep within moments.

Standing next to a tall thin man with short hair, she watched as thousands of warriors followed groups of men carrying ladders across the fields toward the castle walls. As she started to walk away, the white haired man thrust his birch walking stick in her path.

In stark contrast to her guide, a large, fat man with unruly black hair atop a large black Clydesdale horse rode a few feet in front of her. His saddle was a dark wolf hide. A bellowing laughter came from deep within emboldening the hard working warriors. The large crossbow machines continued to send large fire tipped arrows into a burning castle.

Aloft across the battlefield flew a large hawk diving and climbing. She felt pride, fear, and compelled to watch the hawk. A moment later her fourteen year-old son, Madison, and the hawk he rode were momentarily hidden by a forest of arrows. Ten arrows had pierced the hawk immobilizing its wings. Uncontrollably gliding toward the moat. Althea emotionally felt water from the large loud splash. She leaned forward. Neither the son nor the hawk resurfaced.

Althea bolted from the forest toward the moat. While running she realized that the Long Bows were not shooting at the invaders—a few threw empty quivers at the advancing marauders. She was close to the moat when an arrow impaled the small of her back. She fell face first into the moat. Her legs were numb and her arms too short to lift her head above the waterline.

Althea's heavy erratic breathing woke Kendrick.

Suddenly she sat up in bed.

"Kendrick, hold me," Althea implored. They embraced for several quiet minutes.

"Are you okay?" Kendrick asked.

"Yes. But I had a devastating vision similar to yours. We must keep this between us. The queen cannot be known to have visions of disaster."

She told him of the influential laughing fat man, their young son riding a large hawk, many thousands of warriors, Manshire running out of arrows, helpless feeling while she drowned, and the tall thin man.

* * *

He seemed unable to create such turmoil. Luxton Pakrimi looked sixteen—a foot taller and a muscular thirty-five pounds more than other thirteen year olds. His shy wide eyes, smooth nose, and large mouth created a perception of innocence, and his big smile complemented the look.

He had become the target of the desperate head master. The open whipping along with the confinement set a tone that kept the other boys in line, particularly the misfits.

It had become worse when Ulster, at the Archbishop's request, re-instated the monthly 'birthday' celebration. The first miniature festival for the twenty-three orphans with June dates was scheduled for the sixteenth.

Trying to coordinate enough cake pieces for two hundred thirty-nine orphans in an eighty-four seat dining area proved to be the edge of insanity.

A line for boys and another for girls formed in the middle between the narrow tables.

Luxton to be fourteen on June twenty-six, gave up his priority position and stepped to the end of the line as an act of defiance. At the end of the girl's line he stood beside Molly—nine, black hair, sweet hazel eyes, an attractive smile, and a crippled leg.

"What is your date?" Luxton asked.

"November twelve," Molly replied. "How long has it been for you?"

She stumbled over a loose floor stone. Luxton caught her and helped her stand.

"I have been here for nine years. It was okay until a few years ago, when Lady Lee died. She would convince the merchants to donate clothing and food."

They advanced another five feet. Molly tripped again.

"I would be honored to carry you to the cake," Luxton said.

"Oh, that would be nice."

Luxton cradled Molly in his arms. "We are about twenty people from cake. I hope they do not run out. Cake is a nice change."

Molly patted Luxton's shoulder, "Thank you. I would probably trip and drop my cake before finding a seat."

"You are welcome."

They were the last two in line and Sister Margret Ann gave her last piece of cake to Molly. Luxton turned Molly toward the head master for his cake; Ulster wrinkled his nose and swallowed hard while swinging cake between Molly and the baking pan. Ulster acquiesced, but averted his gaze.

Molly's reach was a mere inch too short. She caught enough to juggle the corner morsel into Luxton's chest. His belly laugh triggered the release of the collected tensions of two hundred thirty-nine orphans.

A food fight ensued.

The flying white cake reminded Luxton of snow being whisked about by a cold wind.

His laughter, and the frosting splattered on his clothes raised Ulster's ire. The emotional monsoon that preceded Ulster's disciplinary actions meant one thing to Luxton—another public whipping. He set Molly gently on the end of the bench seat before he turned to run. Ulster caught his collar and it ripped away from the shirt—further maddening the head master.

When he slipped on the frosting littered floor, he knew he had lost, again!

* * *

Oscar took a deep breath, stared out the window, and then faced Kendrick. "I knew this day would eventually arrive," he said in a soft tenor. He took a deep breath and released it in a light whistle. "Your mother had a brother. One summer we spent three very long days visiting your uncle Richard. She wanted to see him while she could walk. You were four."

Oscar glanced at the floor for a few moments. "Abbey had a gift. At the time I thought it was craziness. Now I am not so sure. Apparently, she could predict the future, or more accurately she could predict the outcome based on the choices available. She could see ribbons in the sky."

Kendrick interrupted, "I see ribbons occasionally."

"Well, your Uncle Richard, who claimed to have mastered the ability to read the ribbons, claimed that summer you had the gift and it was strong. Being a devout believer in fate and destiny I could not accept his outcomes based on choices; and I would not let Abbey discuss the gift with you. Fear that you would depend on someone, or something, that was not me, tarnished my relationship with Richard."

"Wow." Kendrick wiped his hands through his hair as he looked to the ceiling.

"A morsel of advise from my narrow-mind, be open to different and do not deny your wife her family."

"I think since Althea is the queen..." Kendrick let the reply float away silently like driftwood. "How do you think this information fits into my vision?"

"Uncle Richard is a tall thin man with white hair combed forward to hide his balding. He walks with a long white birch stick—he has a milder version of the disease that crippled your mother. When you mentioned the black ribbon and the short white hair, I felt goose bumps travel up my spine. We should expect a visit from Richard."

Kendrick and Oscar flinched at the knock on the door.

"Captain. There is someone to see you," the sergeant said. "He said I should tell you to take your time, he had fourteen years."

"A tall white haired man that goes by Richard?" Kendrick asked.

"How did you know?" the sergeant replied.

Holding the door for Kendrick to exit the barracks, Oscar asked, "Where is he?"

"Sorry for the misunderstanding. He is waiting at the castle entrance," the sergeant replied.

Walking to the castle Kendrick rubbed his hands and fidgeted with his quiver.

"Why are you so nervous?" Oscar asked.

"I am uncertain," Kendrick replied.

"I should meet Richard alone."

"I will see you tonight at dinner?"

"Yes."

Kendrick turned toward the market and Oscar continued to the main gate.

Richard sat on the main steps leaning against the wall. "Good afternoon, Oscar." Facing the sun, his eyes remained closed.

"Good afternoon, Richard. Welcome to Manshire," He said to the sergeant, "Thank you. I can escort him from here."

"I half expected you would run me out of the village," Richard said.

"Maybe in my younger days. But, my son has taught me to be more accepting of different views and beliefs."

"I had prepared for an emotional challenge from you," Richard said. He smiled. "This is not a deceptive maneuver of some kind?"

"No deception. You can think of it as an apology for forbidding Abbey the freedom to visit her brother at will."

"Thank you, Oscar." Richard opened his eyes.

Oscar offered his hand to help him stand.

"What brings you to Manshire?" Oscar said shaking Richard's hand.

"Manshire's future is bleak and devastating."

Oscar stared at Richard. He has been here maybe ten minutes and the words bleak and devastating are part of the conversation. "How so?" he asked.

"Can we have this conversation in private with Queen Althea and Kendrick?"

"I am again uncomfortable and prefer to hear what you have to say before making any introductions to Althea and Kendrick," Oscar said.

"Please, this one time, believe my intentions are noble. You can always describe me as a lunatic at the end."

Oscar scratched his head and stared at the steps for half a minute. "Come with me."

He asked the maids to leave the Assembly Hall, and then turned his attention to Richard. "I will bring the queen and Kendrick here. I should be about ten minutes."

Oscar arrived with Kendrick and Althea to find Richard lying on the floor. He struggled to stand. "I have a joint disease and lying on the cool floor eases the pain."

Althea gasped and Kendrick covered his mouth with his palm—they looked to each other. "The tall man from my vision," the queen whispered.

"Same man from my vision," Kendrick added.

"Queen Althea, Kendrick, I introduce Richard, my brother-in-law. He has requested an audience with your grace to discuss what he calls a bleak and devastating future."

"This should be interesting," Althea whispered to Kendrick.

"Please be seated," Richard said. He waited for everyone to sit. "Your baby is the last opportunity to prevent the destruction of Manshire."

Kendrick, who was about to speak, noticed Oscar raise his hand to stop him.

"I am providing the following information for the purpose of validating my predictions and ability," Richard continued.

Kendrick leaned forward on a single chair arm. Althea pushed her chair back and sat on the front edge. Oscar leaned forward with his elbows on the table.

"In three days, your son will be a difficult delivery," Richard said. "He will die if the mid-wife's reaction to his sapphire complexion is slow. If he dies, Manshire will also die. The following morning his birthmark, a brownish oval discoloration will appear on his right shoulder."

Watching Richard furtively with narrowed eyes," You simply could be lucky with those predictions. If you have predictive abilities, will my son and I survive?" Althea asked.

Oscar turned quickly to assess Richard's reaction.

"The child will arrive when the moon passes the sun and a fleeting darkness covers Manshire. He will be the only brightness."

"When does our son become the last opportunity? If your predictions are true regarding the birth, can you provide the same clarity about the fate of Manshire as it is related to the baby?" Kendrick asked.

Oscar surprised by Kendrick's reaction wished he had taken their vision discussion more seriously.

"Fate will not determine the outcome. If it did we could only wait for Manshire to fall. There are scarce opportunities beforehand, but if they are missed, it will fall to him as the last resort. As to when, your son will be fourteen," Richard replied.

"Kendrick and I had similar visions of a vast army attacking and destroying Manshire. Images had similarities and differences. Do the differences represent the opportunities?" Althea asked.

"No. For Kendrick, they will be a quick sensation. For your son, the opportunities will be perceived as another learning experience—he will have no fear, which may place him in grave danger. For you, recognition will always be too late," Richard replied.

"What can you tell us about the scarce opportunities?" Oscar asked.

Richard smiled. "They are the result of decisions made by others along the way. Random and swift best describes their nature." Richard nodded to Oscar. "At this moment, here is what I can tell you about the last opportunity. Your recent past meets a powerful future. A false one becomes thousands. An ancient bird will save your son from the moat. Thousands of invaders will come from the east after traveling six years.

Andean White

After family, Sage the dog, and biking, writing is my joy.

My career as a small business owner was cut short by Parkinson's Disease. After the decision to sell the business was made, it became apparent that few of the buyers knew how to develop a business plan. Writing an e-book on "How to Purchase a Small Business" seemed so logical. It was a good guide with lists of questions and a sample business plan. But marketing it became another matter.

A new hobby of writing travel journals, sprinkled with a little encouragement from family and friends, sparked a desire to test my writing skills, and decided it was time for that dream job—coffee on the deck, smokin' keyboard, e-books zooming through the Internet, and dollars collecting in the bank account.

Early spy short stories were posted on free e-book sites and developed a small following, which I thought was large enough to attempt a book. That second book was disappointing, but the experience was invaluable. And, I knew I wanted to write.

I fell back on my small business experience, and surrounded myself with the best people.

Two years later, I was an aspiring writer, telling stories that hopefully guide a reader's imagination to a world of excitement, and provide a brief rest from everyday duties.

I discovered that true writing was hard work, and quality required a lot of detail awareness. Maybe, there was still a chance of coffee on the deck...someday.

As a young boy at family gatherings, I recall listening to the men after a meal. The opinions around the subjects of politics, car brands, hippies, and rock n roll filled the room with energy like aromatic smoke from a pipe. But, when the story telling began everyone found a seat or patch of floor. We sat for hours laughing and gasping at the stories, fact or fiction—they shaped who we became and it strengthened our imaginations. Fifty years later, it's clear, a world without imagination would be pretty boring.

Marrying my high school sweetheart was my most brilliant accomplishment. We enjoy sporting events, backyard barbeques, outdoors, concerts, and traveling with our friends.

Parkinson's Disease donation

1.0% to 1.5% of the population has Parkinson's disease—odds are someone on your street has Parkinson's.

Statistically, one, two, maybe three people on most major flights are affected with Parkinson's. A concert of 20,000 people will have 200 to 300 patients struggling daily with a disease that reveals itself in a long list of debilitating symptoms. The most visible is a shaking hand, chin, arm, leg, or foot.

20% of all profits will be donated to Parkinson's disease research.

www.ingramcontent.com/pod-product-compliance
Lightning Source LLC
Chambersburg PA
CBHW070748180626
46818CB00007B/3033